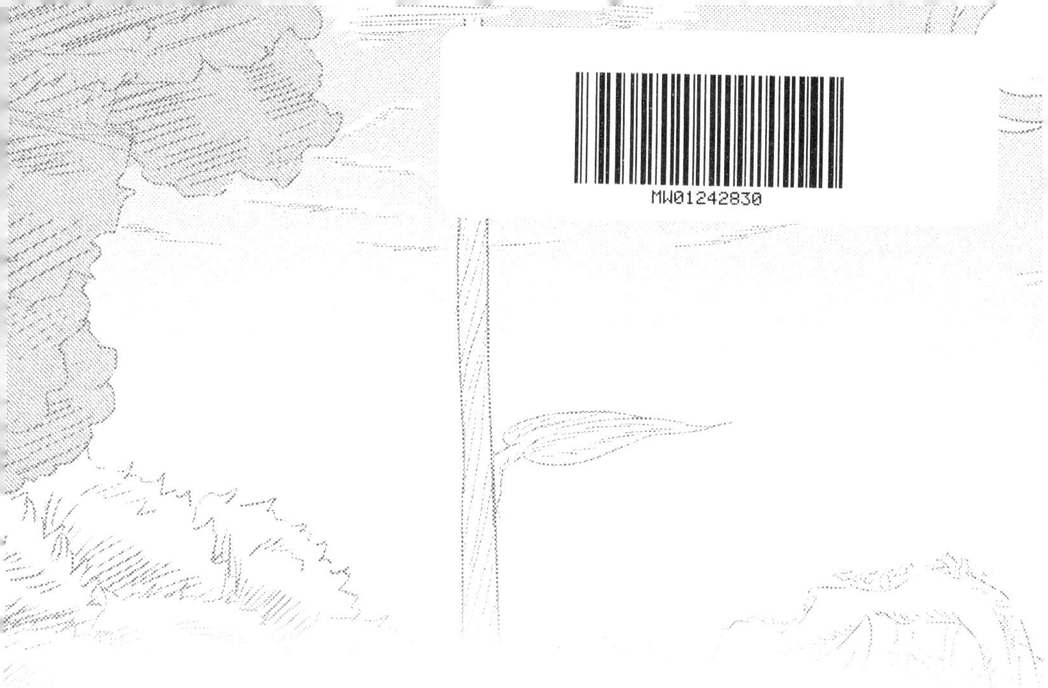

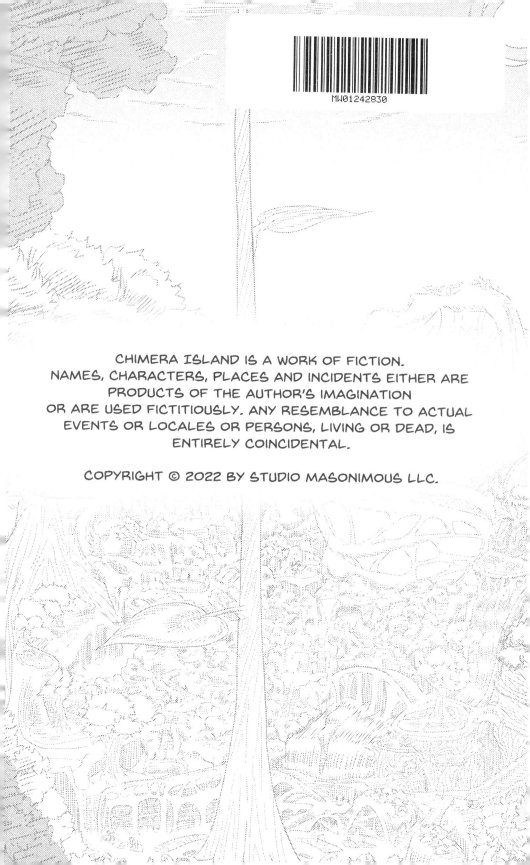

CHIMERA ISLAND IS A WORK OF FICTION.
NAMES, CHARACTERS, PLACES AND INCIDENTS EITHER ARE PRODUCTS OF THE AUTHOR'S IMAGINATION OR ARE USED FICTITIOUSLY. ANY RESEMBLANCE TO ACTUAL EVENTS OR LOCALES OR PERSONS, LIVING OR DEAD, IS ENTIRELY COINCIDENTAL.

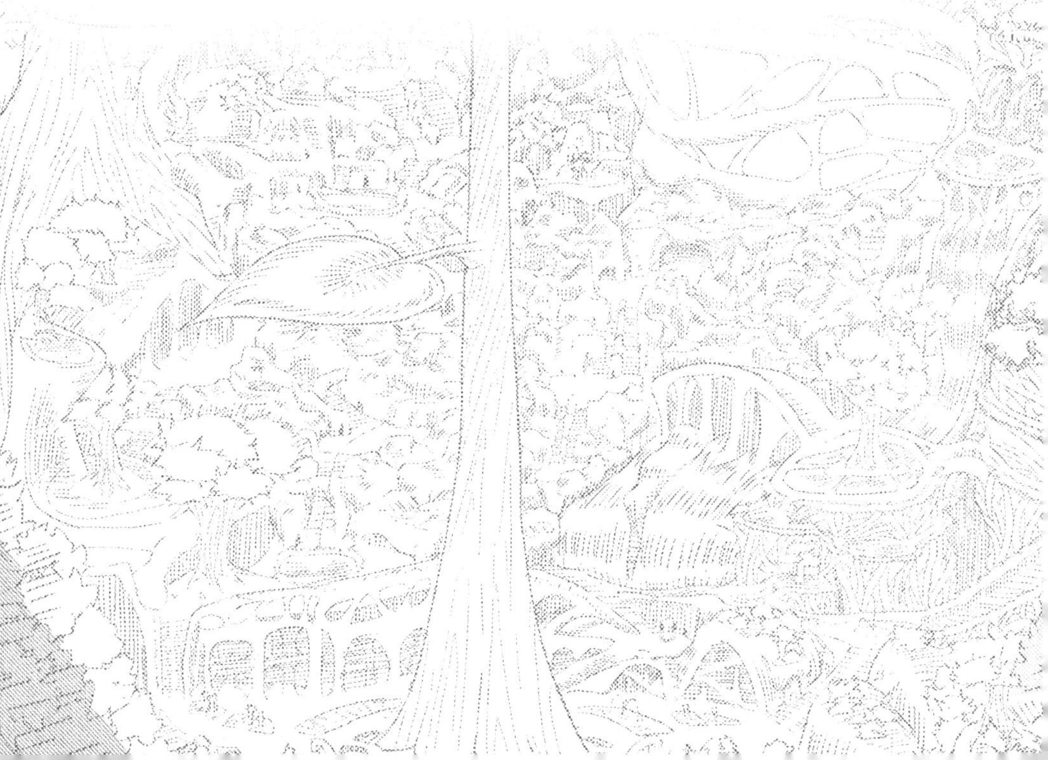

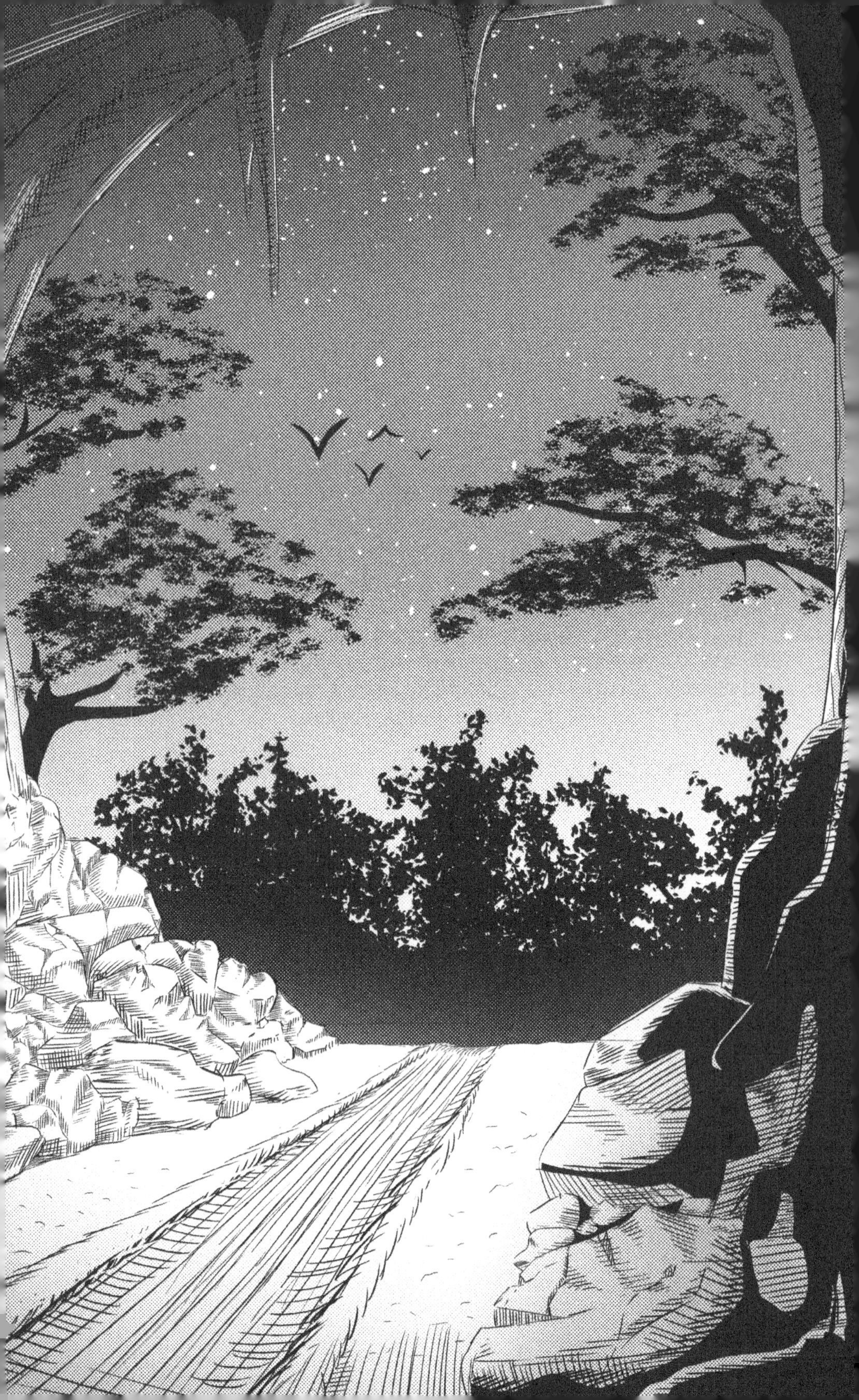

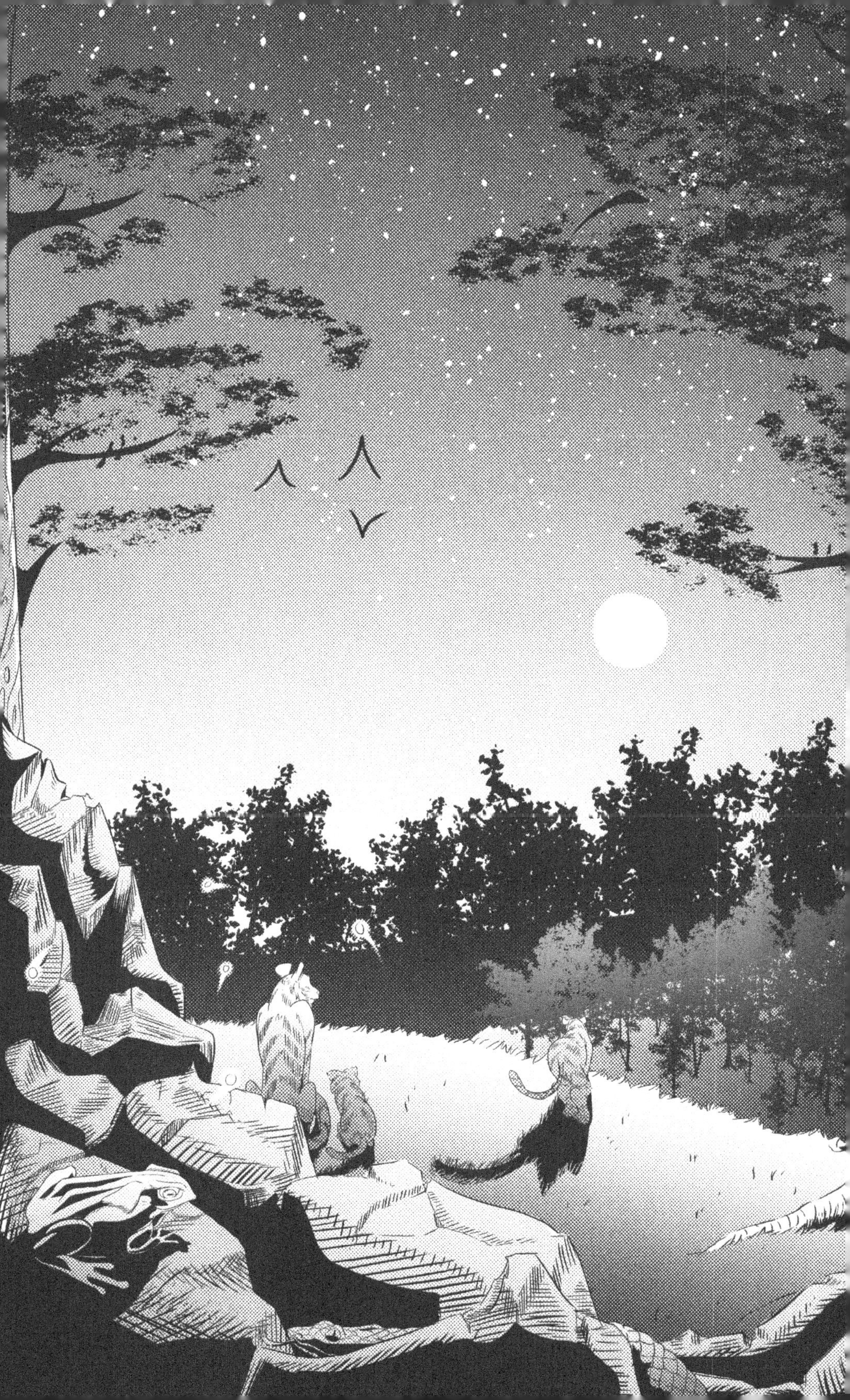

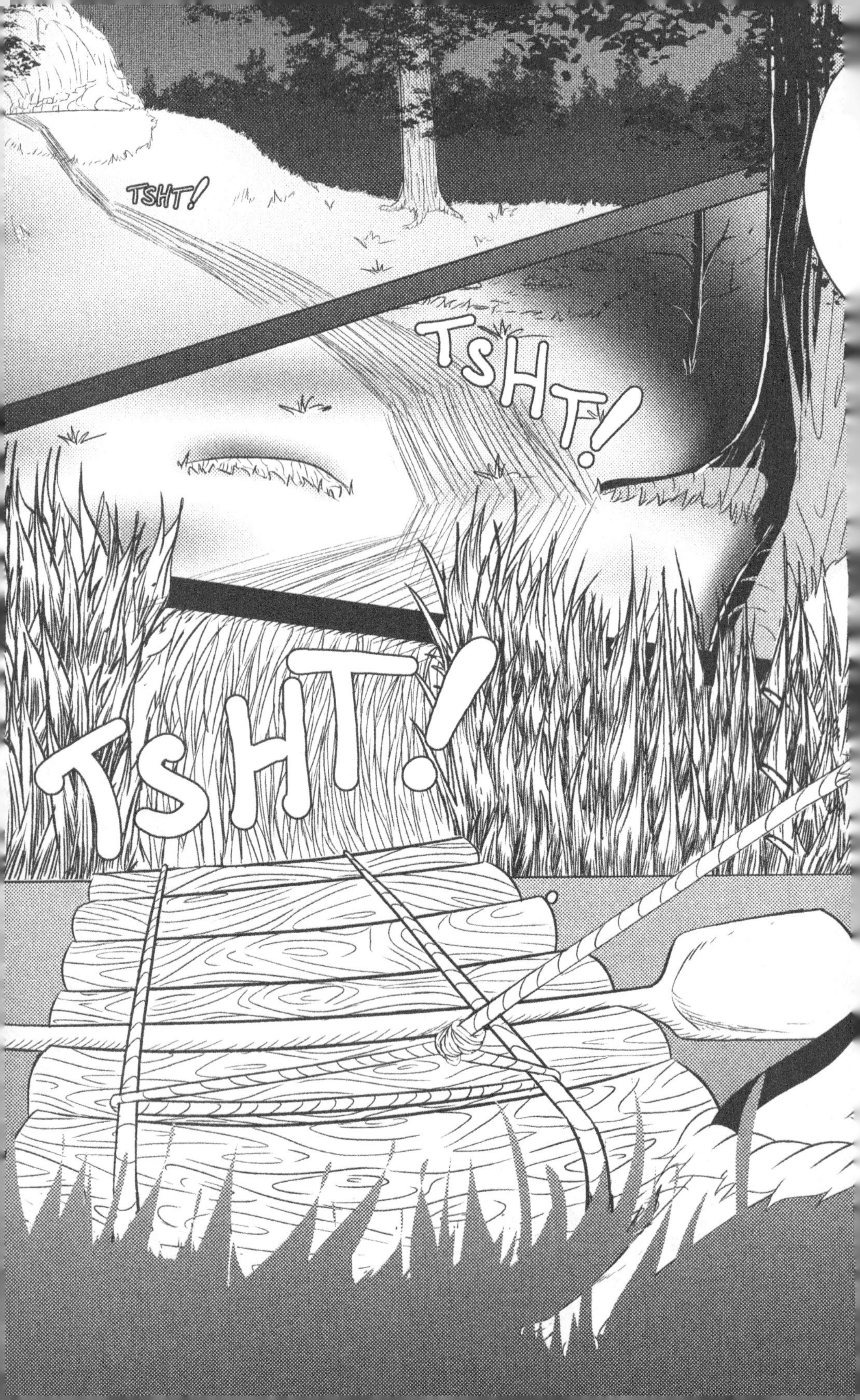
TSHT!
TSHT!
TSHT!

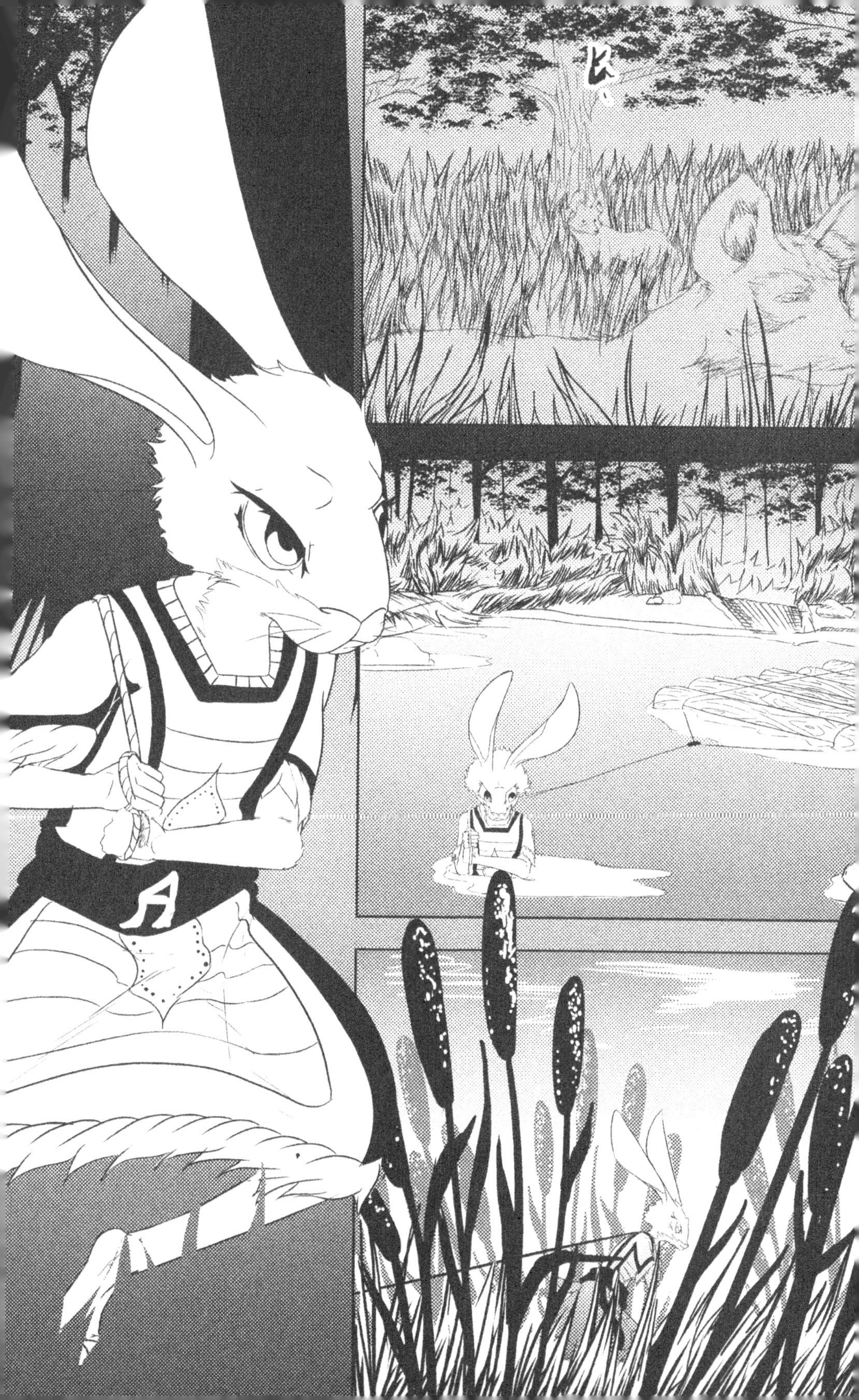
ヒ、

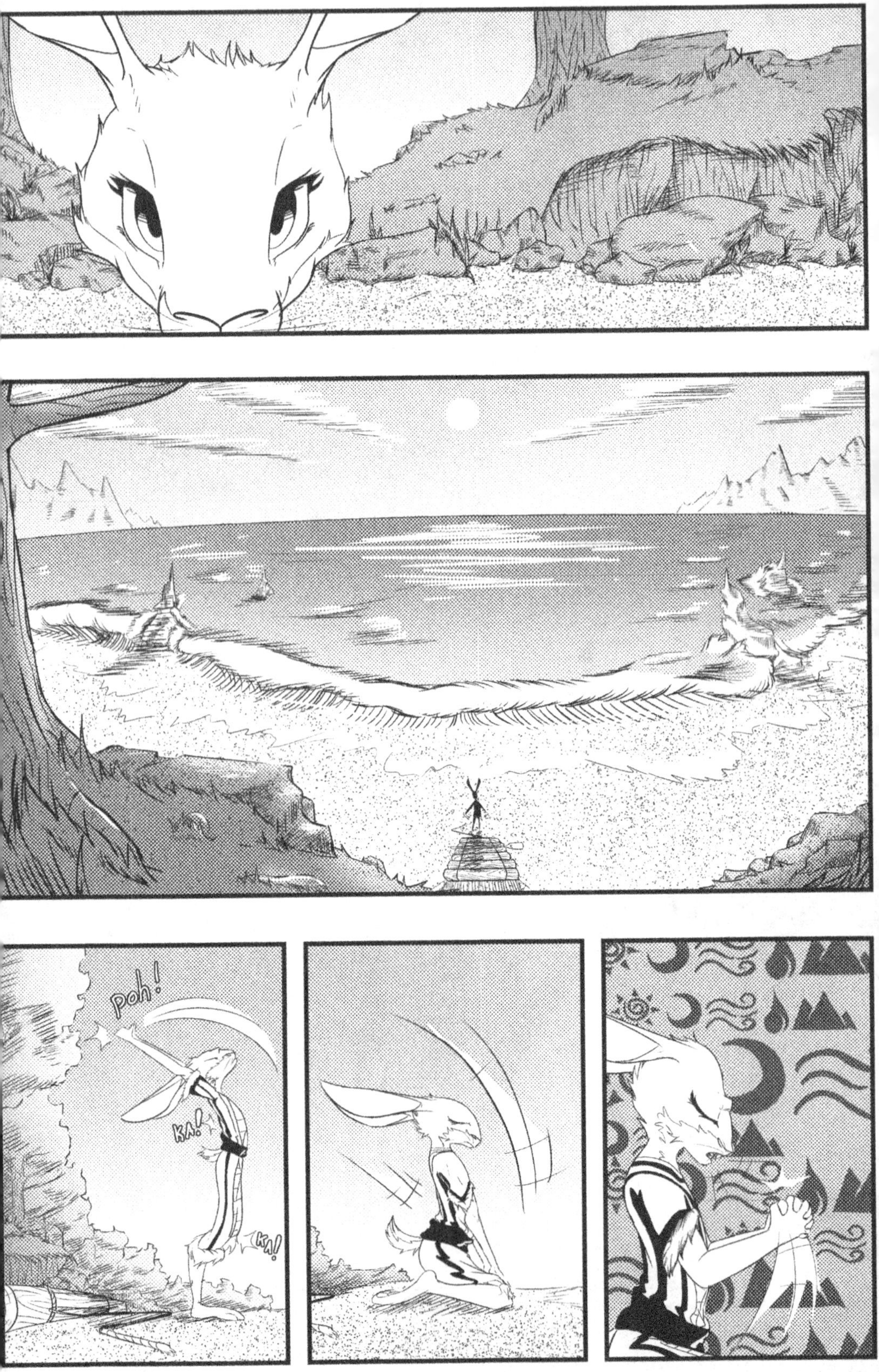
poh!
KA!
KA!

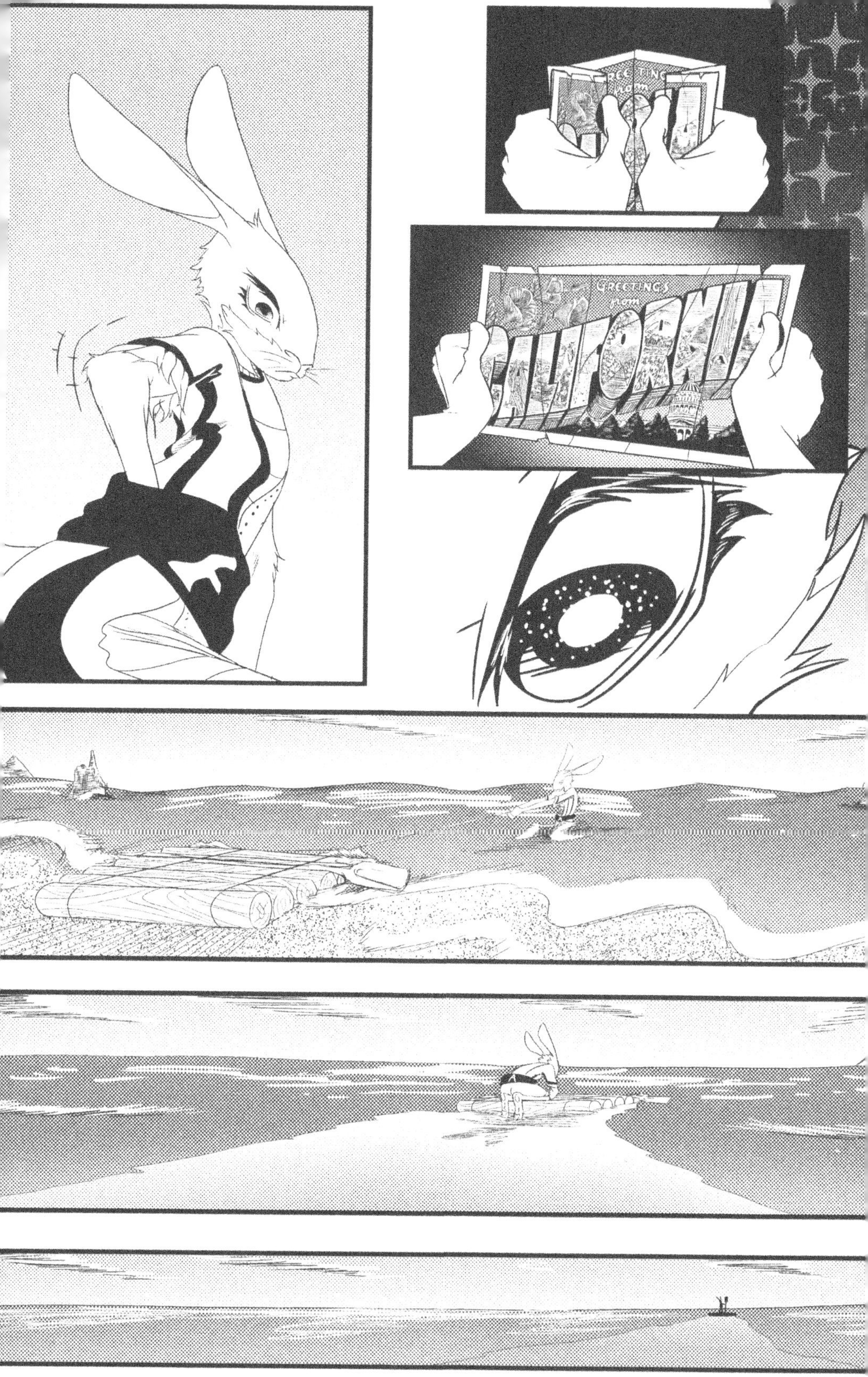
GREETINGS from

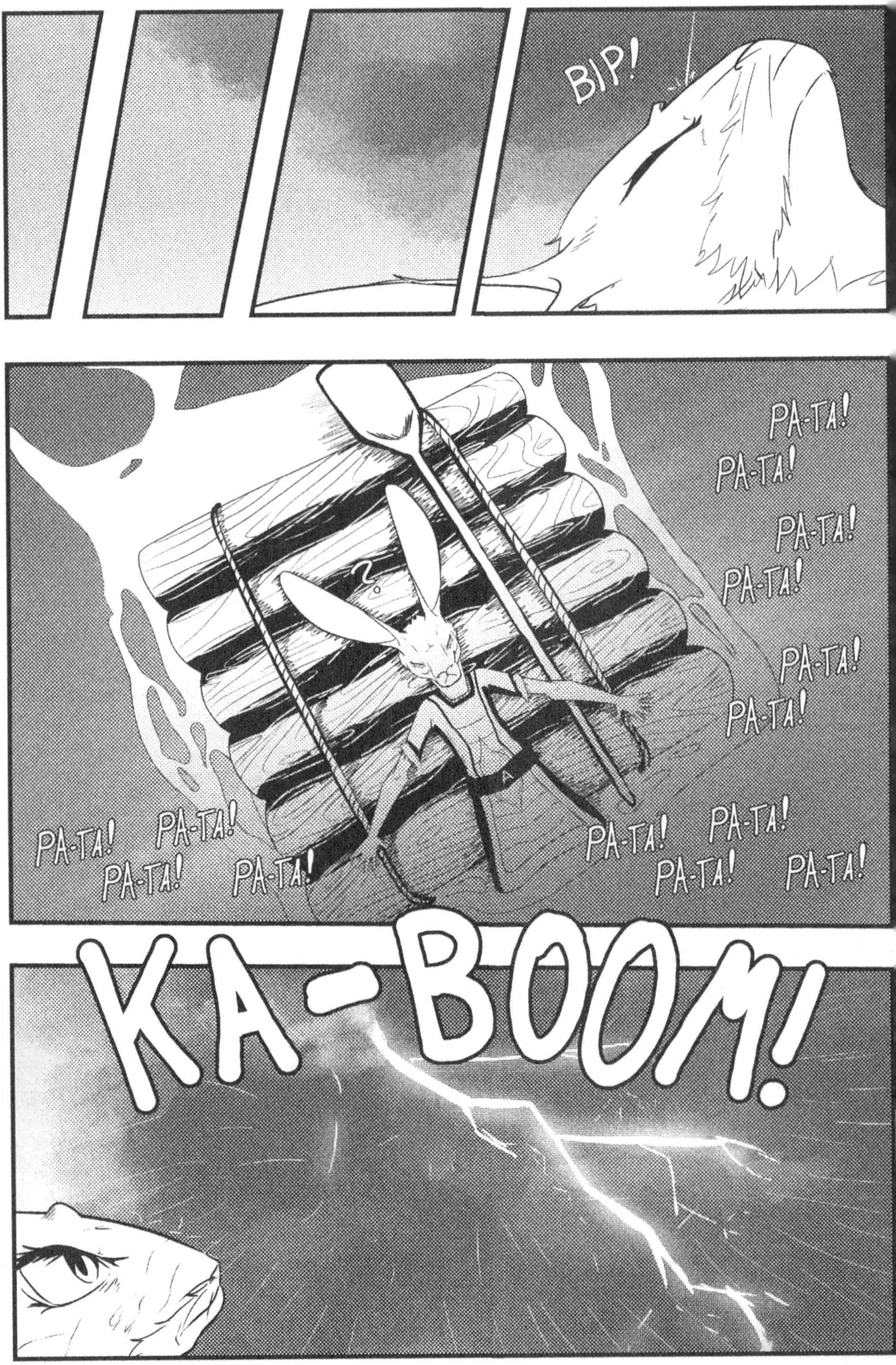
BIP!
?
PA-TA!
PA-TA!
PA-TA!
PA-TA!
PA-TA!
PA-TA!
PA-TA!
PA-TA!
PA-TA!
PA-TA!
PA-TA!
PA-TA!
PA-TA!
PA-TA!
KA-BOOM!

TA!
TA!
TA!
TA!
TA!
DA-
DUM!!
SPOOSH!!

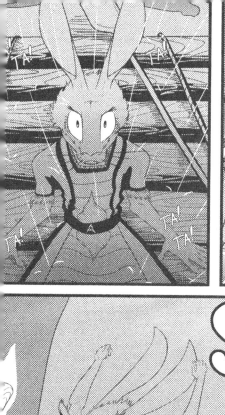

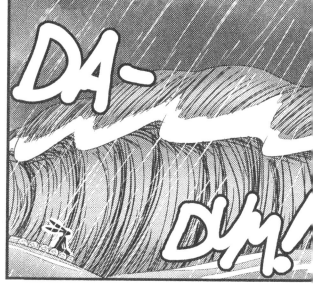

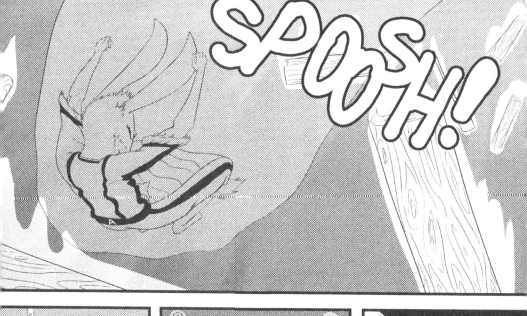

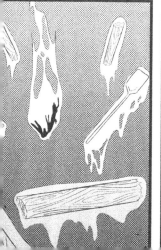

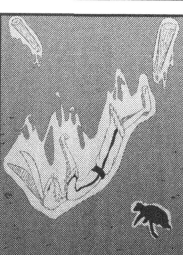

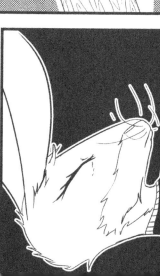

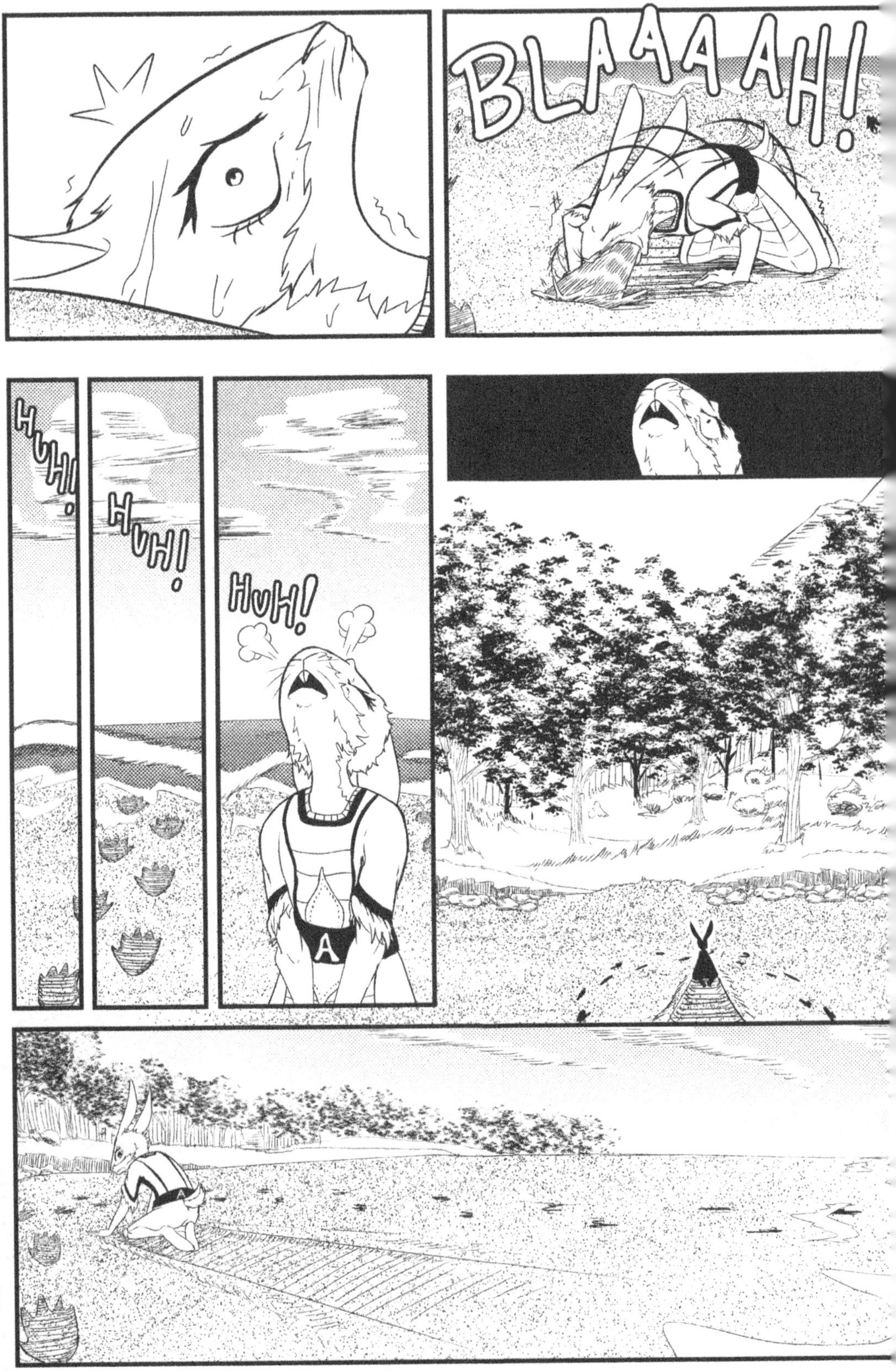
BLAAAAH!
HUH!
HUH!
HUH!

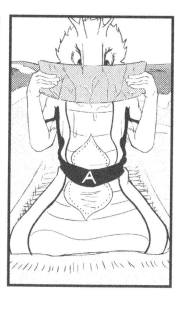

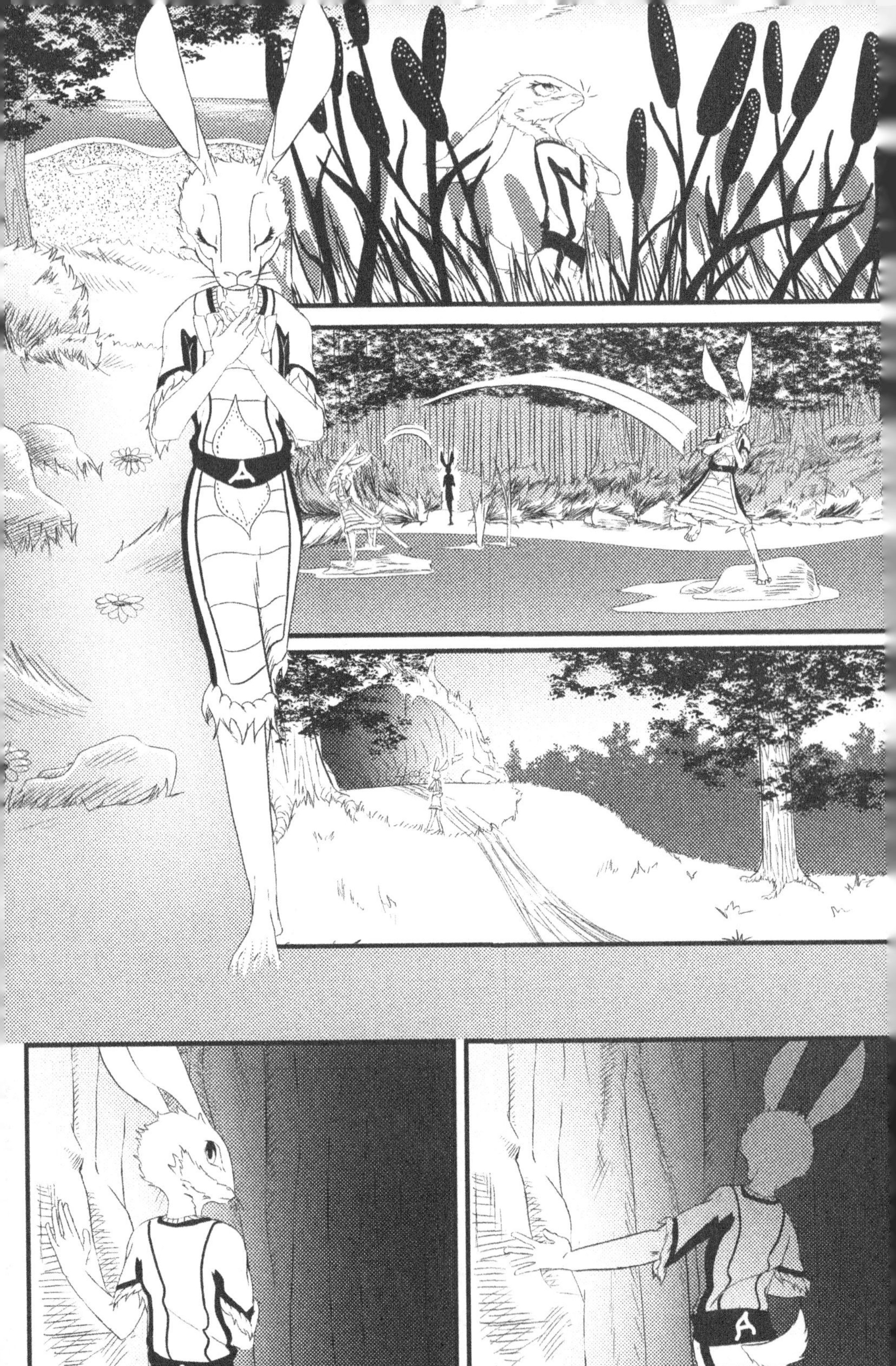

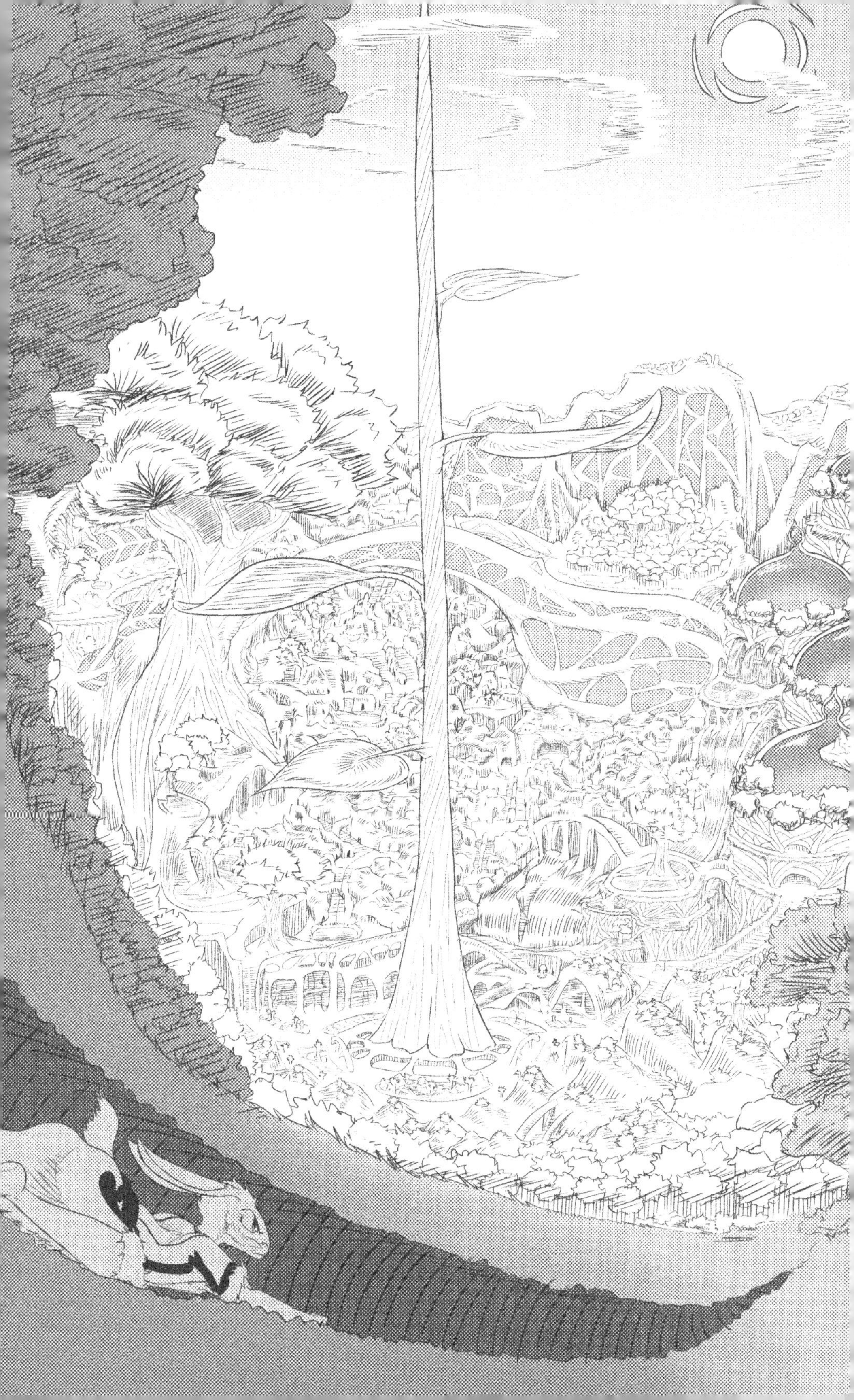

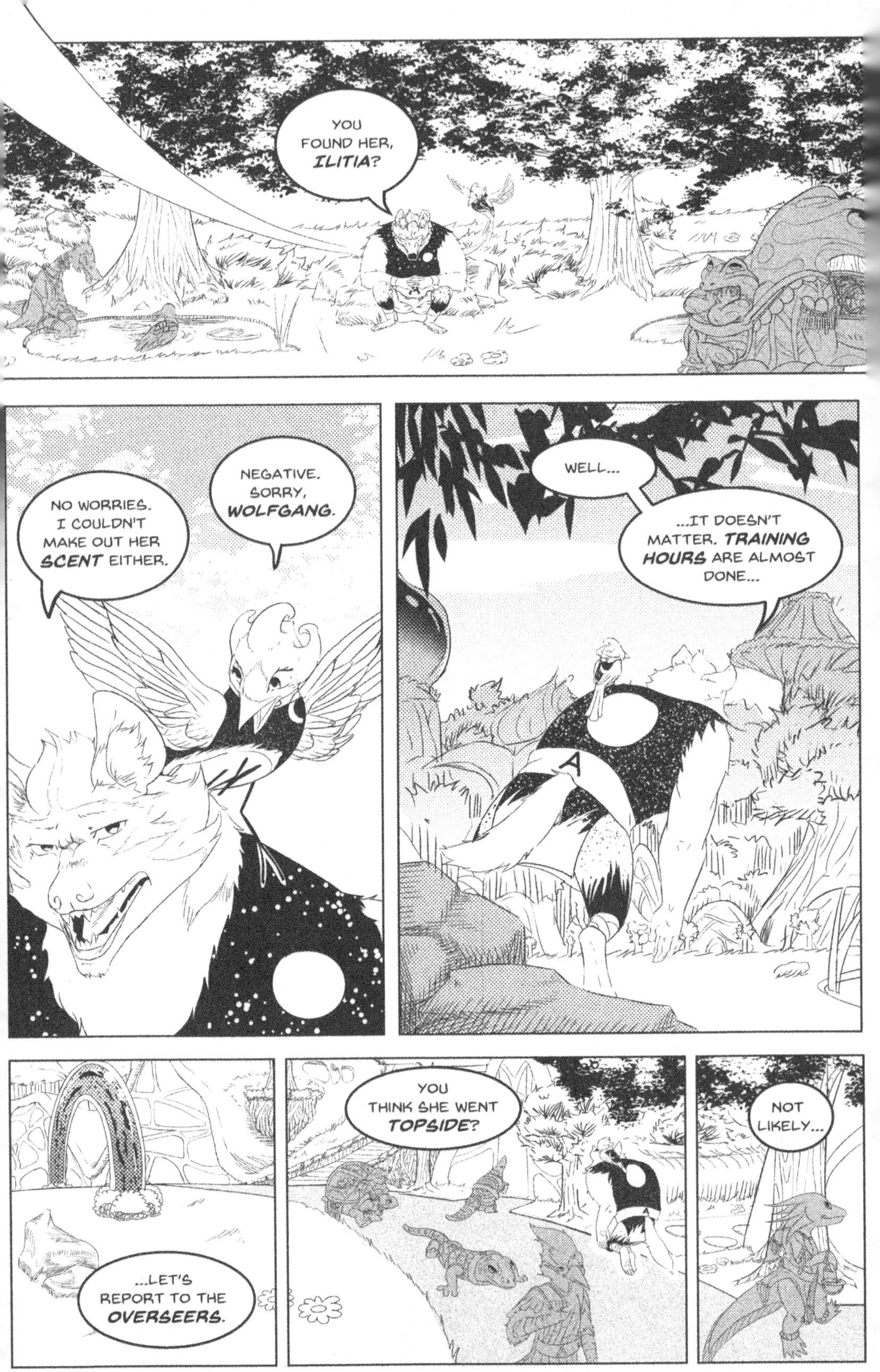
YOU FOUND HER, ILITIA?
NO WORRIES. I COULDN'T MAKE OUT HER SCENT EITHER.
NEGATIVE. SORRY, WOLFGANG.
WELL...
...IT DOESN'T MATTER. TRAINING HOURS ARE ALMOST DONE...
...LET'S REPORT TO THE OVERSEERS.
YOU THINK SHE WENT TOPSIDE?
NOT LIKELY...

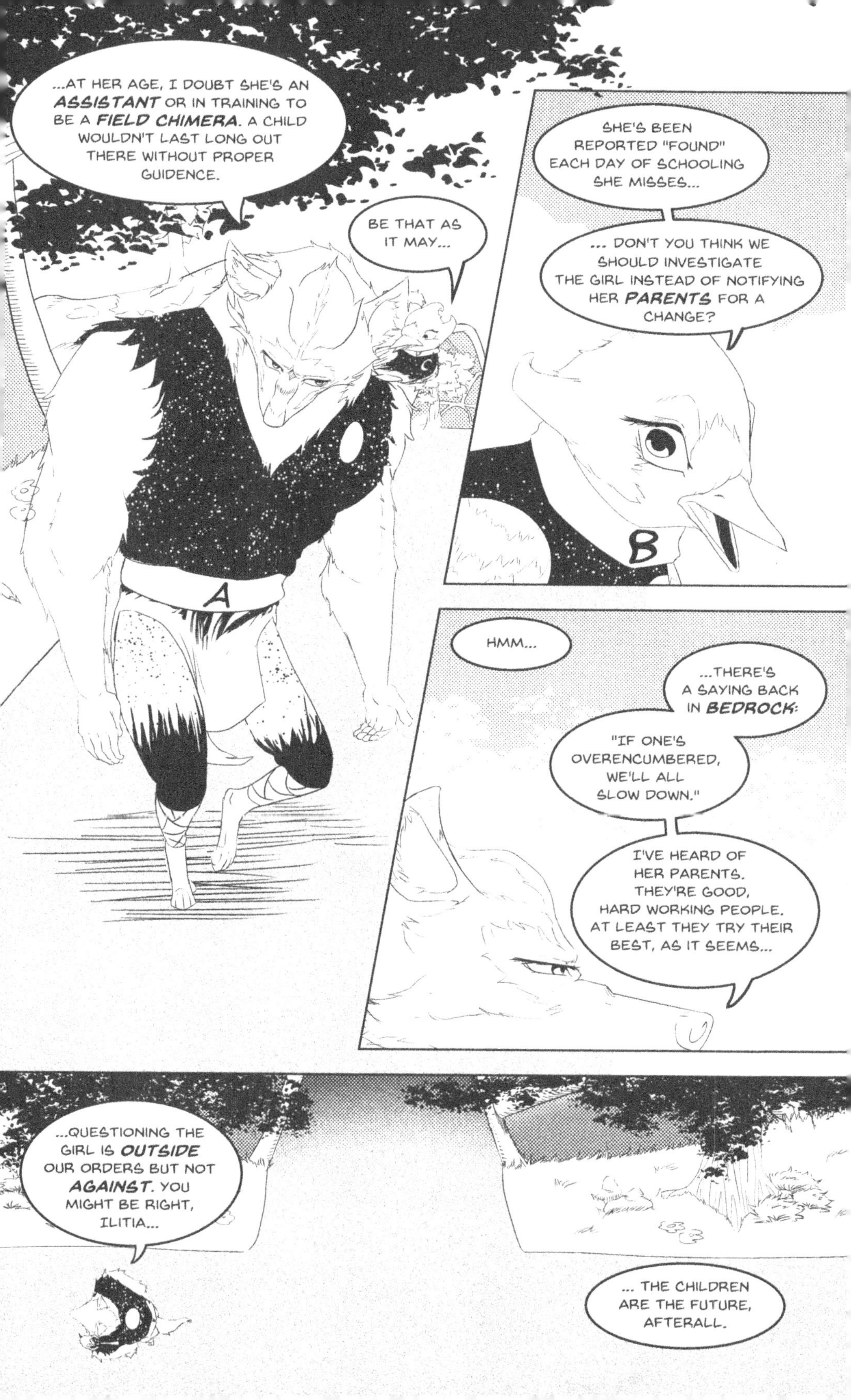
...AT HER AGE, I DOUBT SHE'S AN ASSISTANT OR IN TRAINING TO BE A FIELD CHIMERA. A CHILD WOULDN'T LAST LONG OUT THERE WITHOUT PROPER GUIDENCE.
BE THAT AS IT MAY...
A
SHE'S BEEN REPORTED "FOUND" EACH DAY OF SCHOOLING SHE MISSES...
... DON'T YOU THINK WE SHOULD INVESTIGATE THE GIRL INSTEAD OF NOTIFYING HER PARENTS FOR A CHANGE?
B
HMM...
...THERE'S A SAYING BACK IN BEDROCK:
"IF ONE'S OVERENCUMBERED, WE'LL ALL SLOW DOWN."
I'VE HEARD OF HER PARENTS. THEY'RE GOOD, HARD WORKING PEOPLE. AT LEAST THEY TRY THEIR BEST, AS IT SEEMS...
...QUESTIONING THE GIRL IS OUTSIDE OUR ORDERS BUT NOT AGAINST. YOU MIGHT BE RIGHT, ILITIA...
... THE CHILDREN ARE THE FUTURE, AFTERALL.

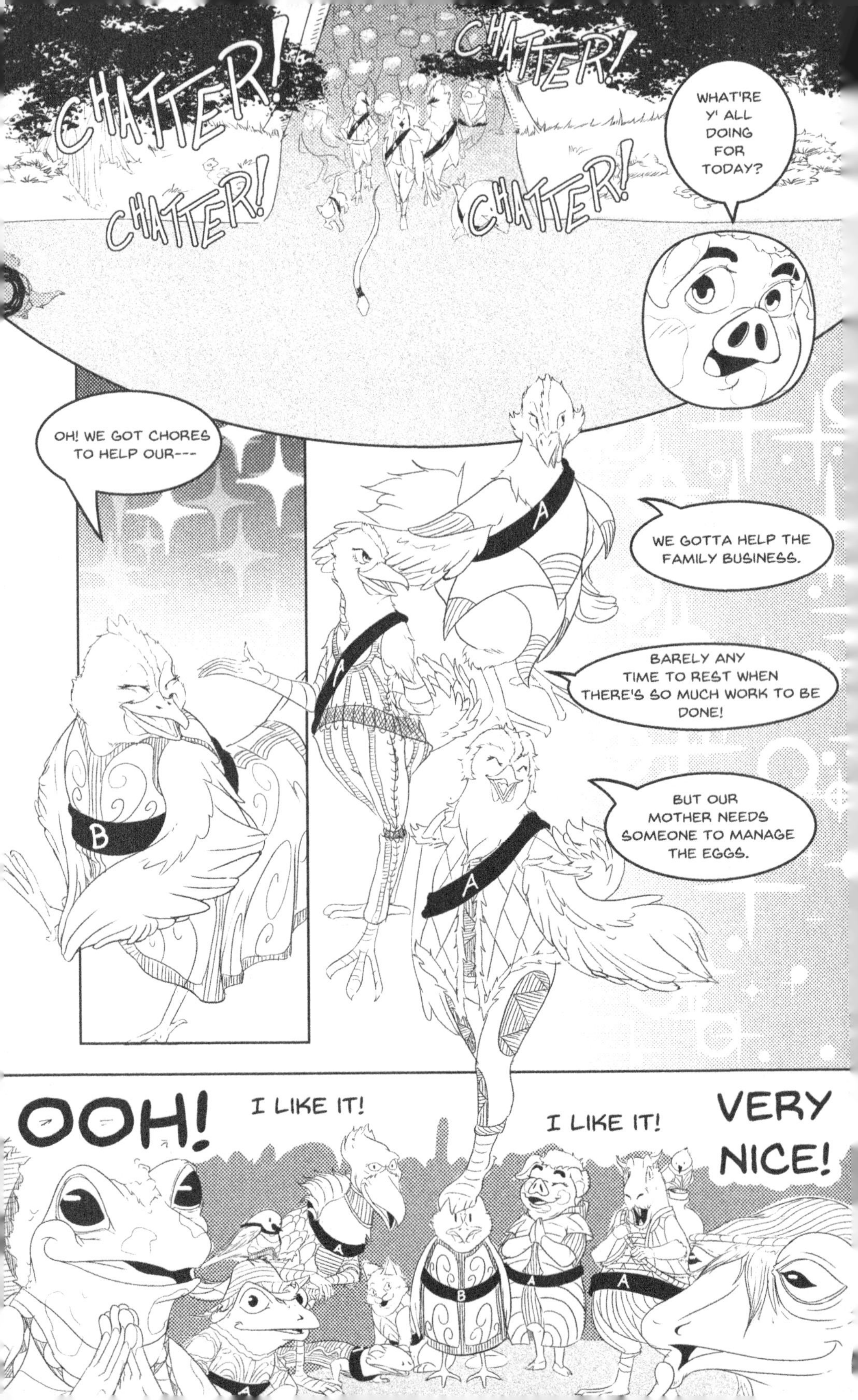
CHATTER!
CHATTER!
CHATTER!
CHATTER!
WHAT'RE Y' ALL DOING FOR TODAY?
OH! WE GOT CHORES TO HELP OUR---
WE GOTTA HELP THE FAMILY BUSINESS.
BARELY ANY TIME TO REST WHEN THERE'S SO MUCH WORK TO BE DONE!
BUT OUR MOTHER NEEDS SOMEONE TO MANAGE THE EGGS.
OOH!
I LIKE IT!
I LIKE IT!
VERY NICE!

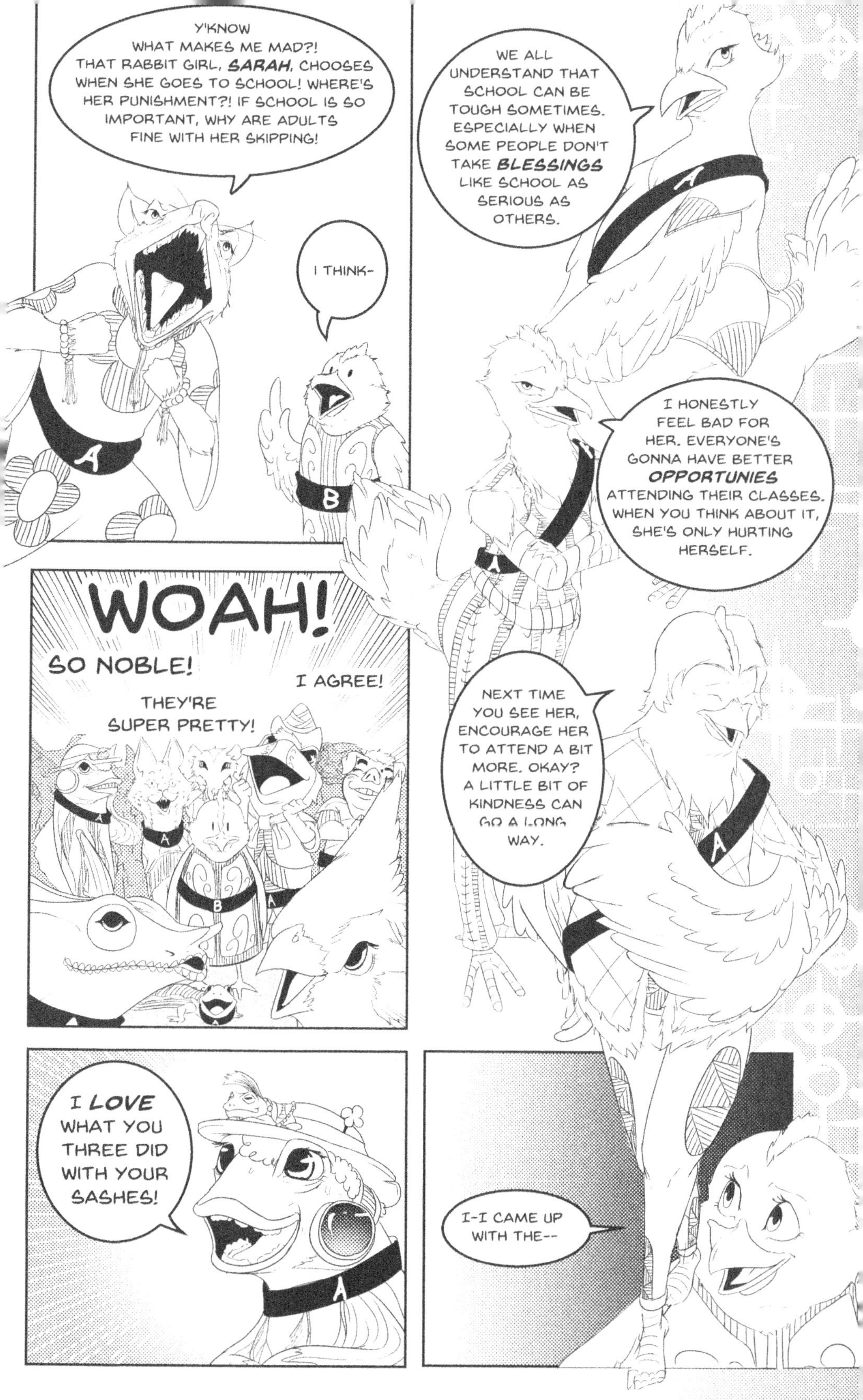
Y'KNOW WHAT MAKES ME MAD?! THAT RABBIT GIRL, SARAH, CHOOSES WHEN SHE GOES TO SCHOOL! WHERE'S HER PUNISHMENT?! IF SCHOOL IS SO IMPORTANT, WHY ARE ADULTS FINE WITH HER SKIPPING!
I THINK-
WE ALL UNDERSTAND THAT SCHOOL CAN BE TOUGH SOMETIMES. ESPECIALLY WHEN SOME PEOPLE DON'T TAKE BLESSINGS LIKE SCHOOL AS SERIOUS AS OTHERS.
I HONESTLY FEEL BAD FOR HER. EVERYONE'S GONNA HAVE BETTER OPPORTUNIES ATTENDING THEIR CLASSES. WHEN YOU THINK ABOUT IT, SHE'S ONLY HURTING HERSELF.
WOAH!
SO NOBLE!
I AGREE!
THEY'RE SUPER PRETTY!
NEXT TIME YOU SEE HER, ENCOURAGE HER TO ATTEND A BIT MORE. OKAY? A LITTLE BIT OF KINDNESS CAN GO A LONG WAY.
I LOVE WHAT YOU THREE DID WITH YOUR SASHES!
I-I CAME UP WITH THE--

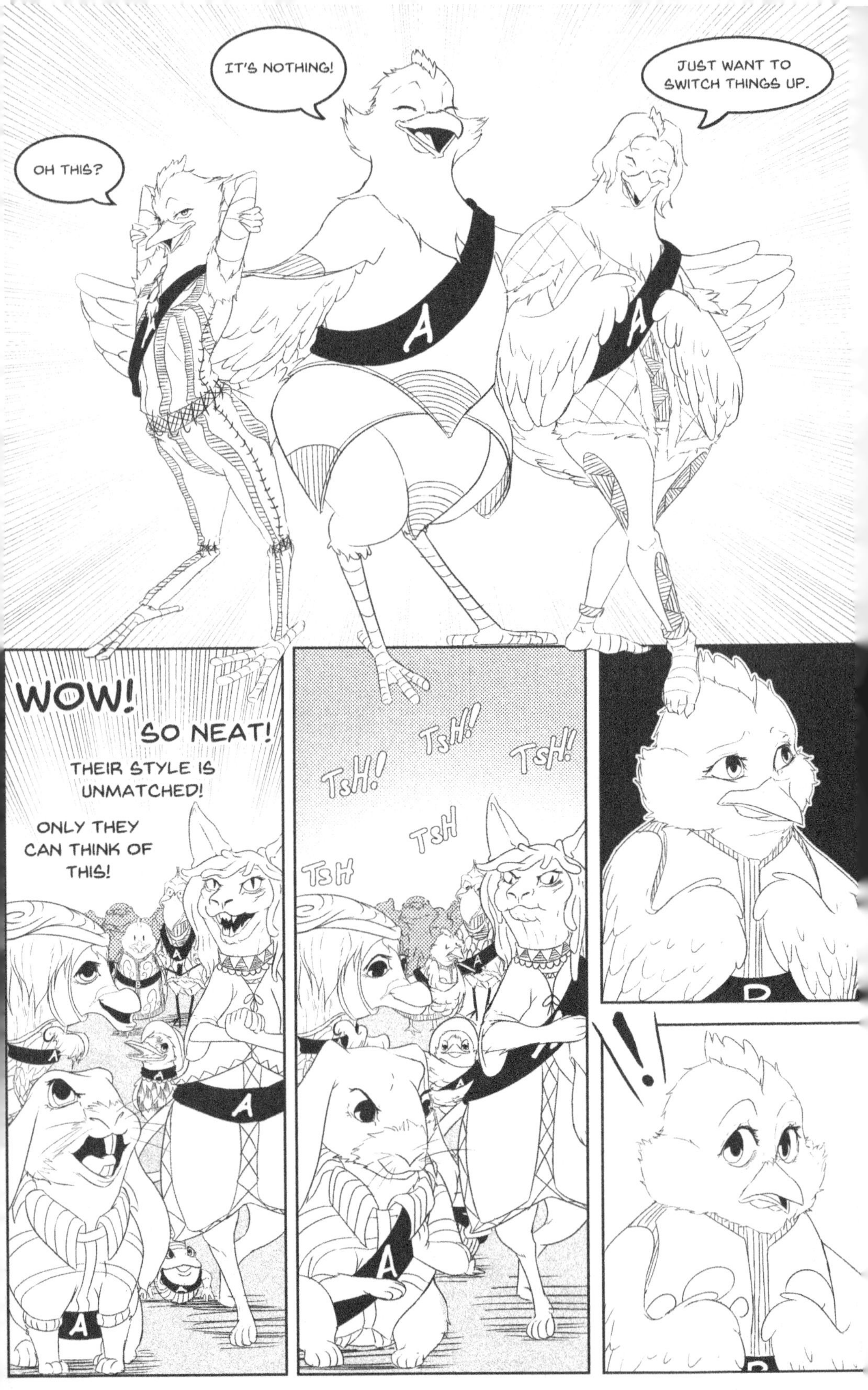
OH THIS?
IT'S NOTHING!
JUST WANT TO SWITCH THINGS UP.
WOW!
SO NEAT!
THEIR STYLE IS UNMATCHED!
ONLY THEY CAN THINK OF THIS!
TsH!
TsH!
TsH!
TsH
TsH
!!

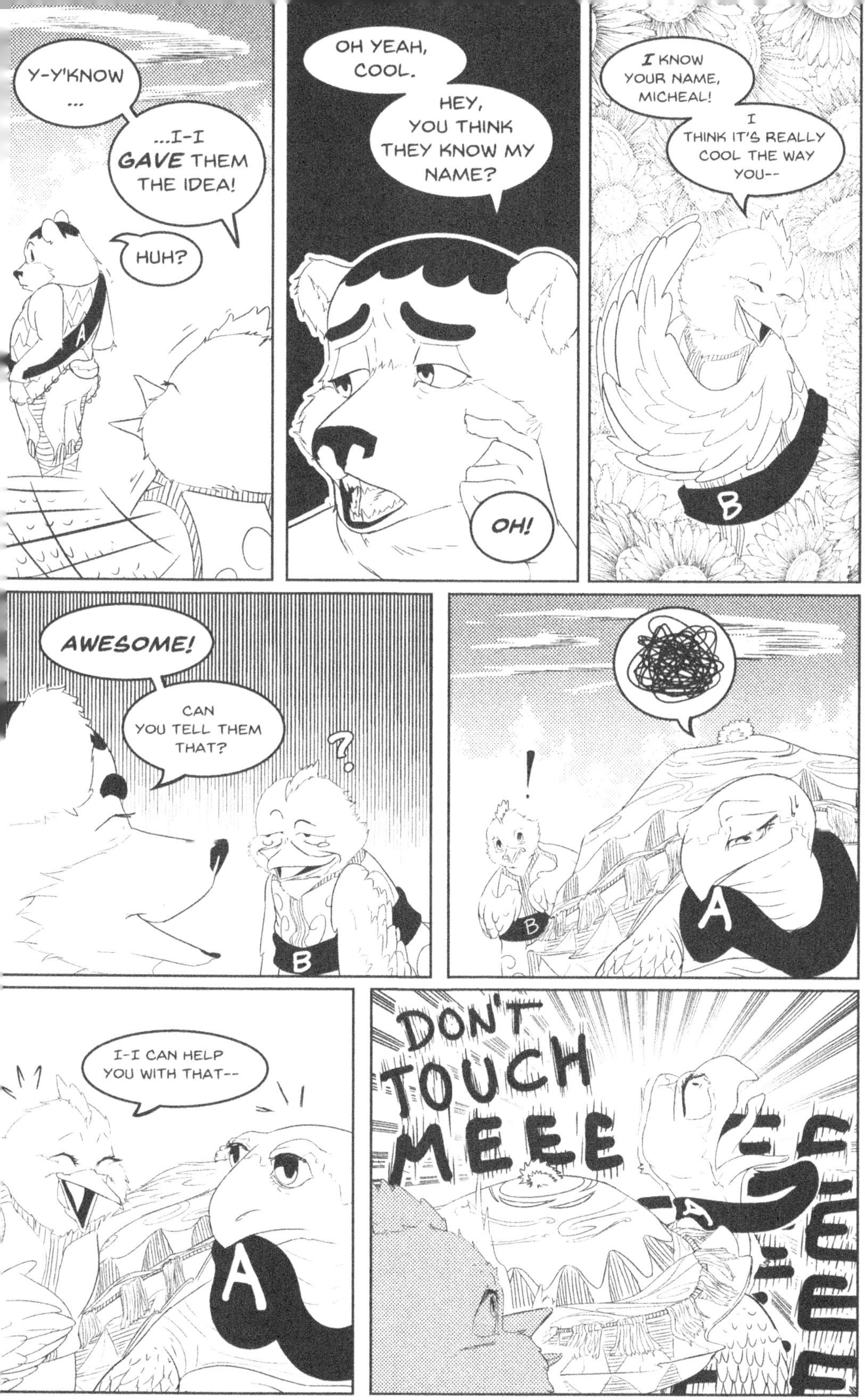

Y-Y'KNOW ...
...I-I **GAVE** THEM THE IDEA!
HUH?
OH YEAH, COOL.
HEY, YOU THINK THEY KNOW MY NAME?
OH!
I KNOW YOUR NAME, MICHEAL!
I THINK IT'S REALLY COOL THE WAY YOU--
AWESOME!
CAN YOU TELL THEM THAT?
?
!
I-I CAN HELP YOU WITH THAT--
DON'T TOUCH MEEE

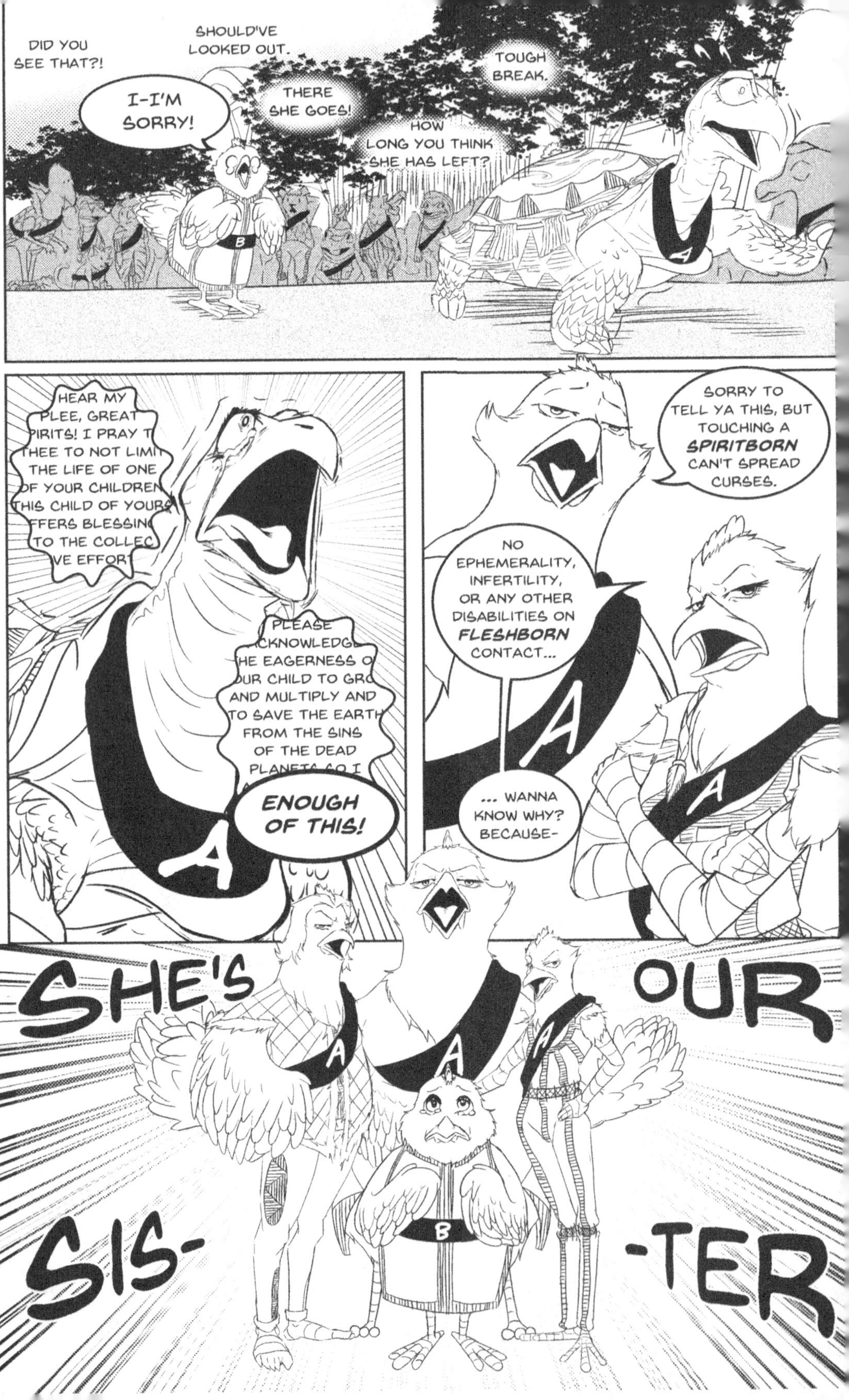
DID YOU SEE THAT?!
SHOULD'VE LOOKED OUT.
I-I'M SORRY!
THERE SHE GOES!
TOUGH BREAK.
HOW LONG YOU THINK SHE HAS LEFT?
HEAR MY PLEE, GREAT PIRITS! I PRAY T THEE TO NOT LIMI THE LIFE OF ONE OF YOUR CHILDREN THIS CHILD OF YOUR FFERS BLESSIN TO THE COLLEC VE EFFOR
PLEASE CKNOWLEDG HE EAGERNESS O OUR CHILD TO GR AND MULTIPLY AND TO SAVE THE EARTH FROM THE SINS OF THE DEAD PLANETS SO I
ENOUGH OF THIS!
SORRY TO TELL YA THIS, BUT TOUCHING A SPIRITBORN CAN'T SPREAD CURSES.
NO EPHEMERALITY, INFERTILITY, OR ANY OTHER DISABILITIES ON FLESHBORN CONTACT...
... WANNA KNOW WHY? BECAUSE-
SHE'S OUR SIS- -TER.

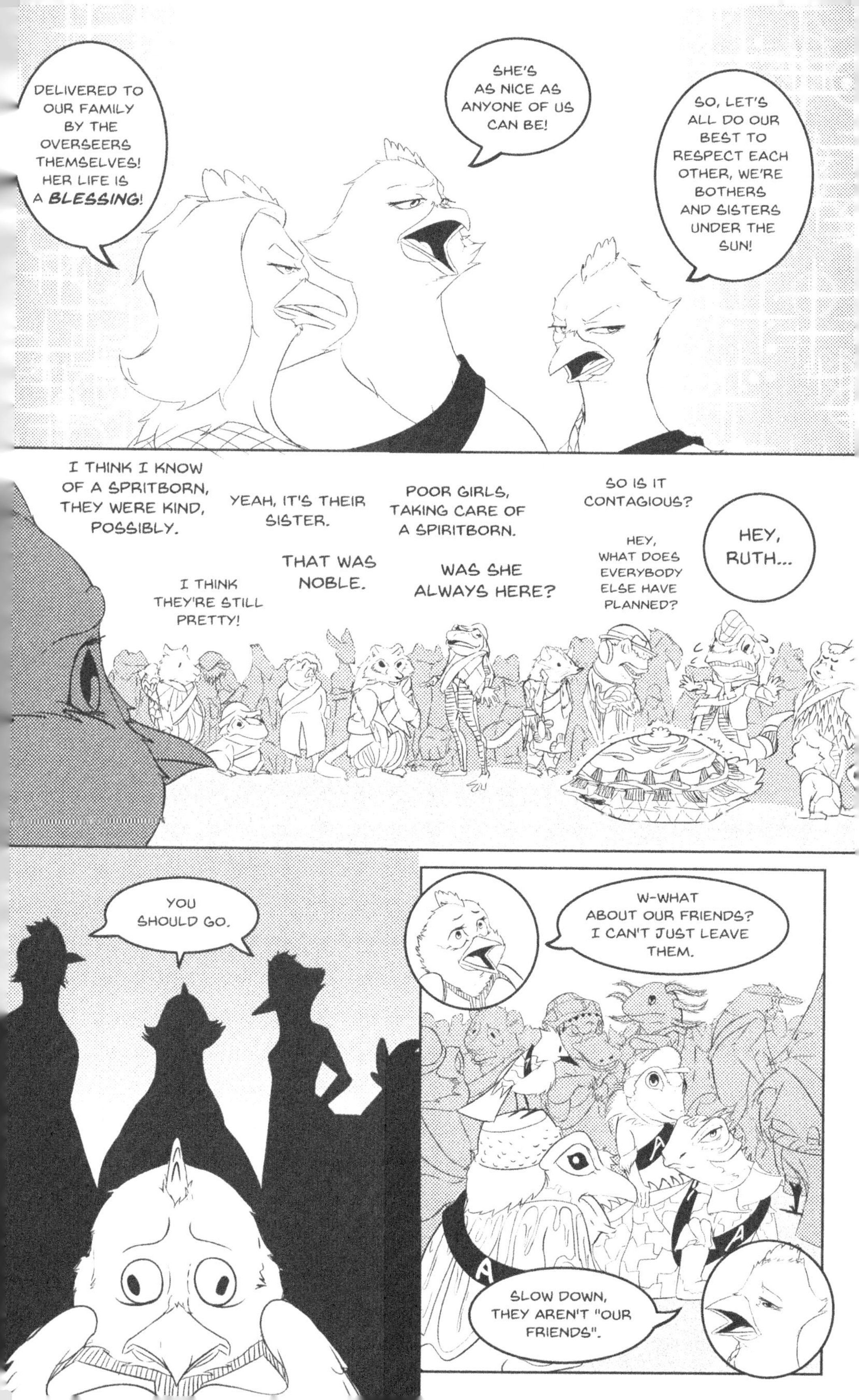
DELIVERED TO OUR FAMILY BY THE OVERSEERS THEMSELVES! HER LIFE IS A *BLESSING*!
SHE'S AS NICE AS ANYONE OF US CAN BE!
SO, LET'S ALL DO OUR BEST TO RESPECT EACH OTHER, WE'RE BOTHERS AND SISTERS UNDER THE SUN!
I THINK I KNOW OF A SPRITBORN, THEY WERE KIND, POSSIBLY.
I THINK THEY'RE STILL PRETTY!
YEAH, IT'S THEIR SISTER.
THAT WAS NOBLE.
POOR GIRLS, TAKING CARE OF A SPIRITBORN.
WAS SHE ALWAYS HERE?
SO IS IT CONTAGIOUS?
HEY, WHAT DOES EVERYBODY ELSE HAVE PLANNED?
HEY, RUTH...
YOU SHOULD GO.
W-WHAT ABOUT OUR FRIENDS? I CAN'T JUST LEAVE THEM.
SLOW DOWN, THEY AREN'T "OUR FRIENDS".

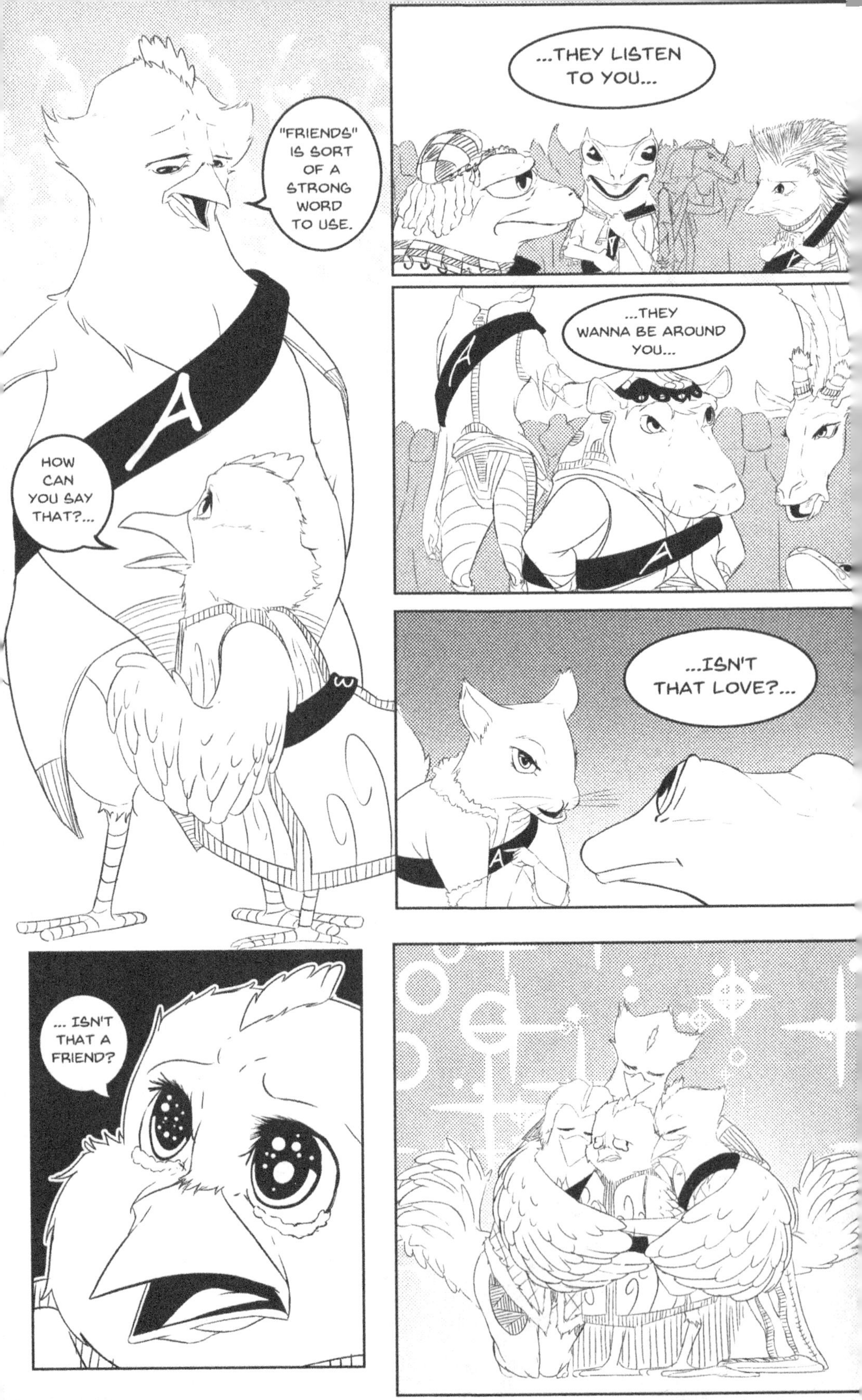
"FRIENDS" IS SORT OF A STRONG WORD TO USE.
HOW CAN YOU SAY THAT?...
...THEY LISTEN TO YOU...
...THEY WANNA BE AROUND YOU...
...ISN'T THAT LOVE?...
... ISN'T THAT A FRIEND?

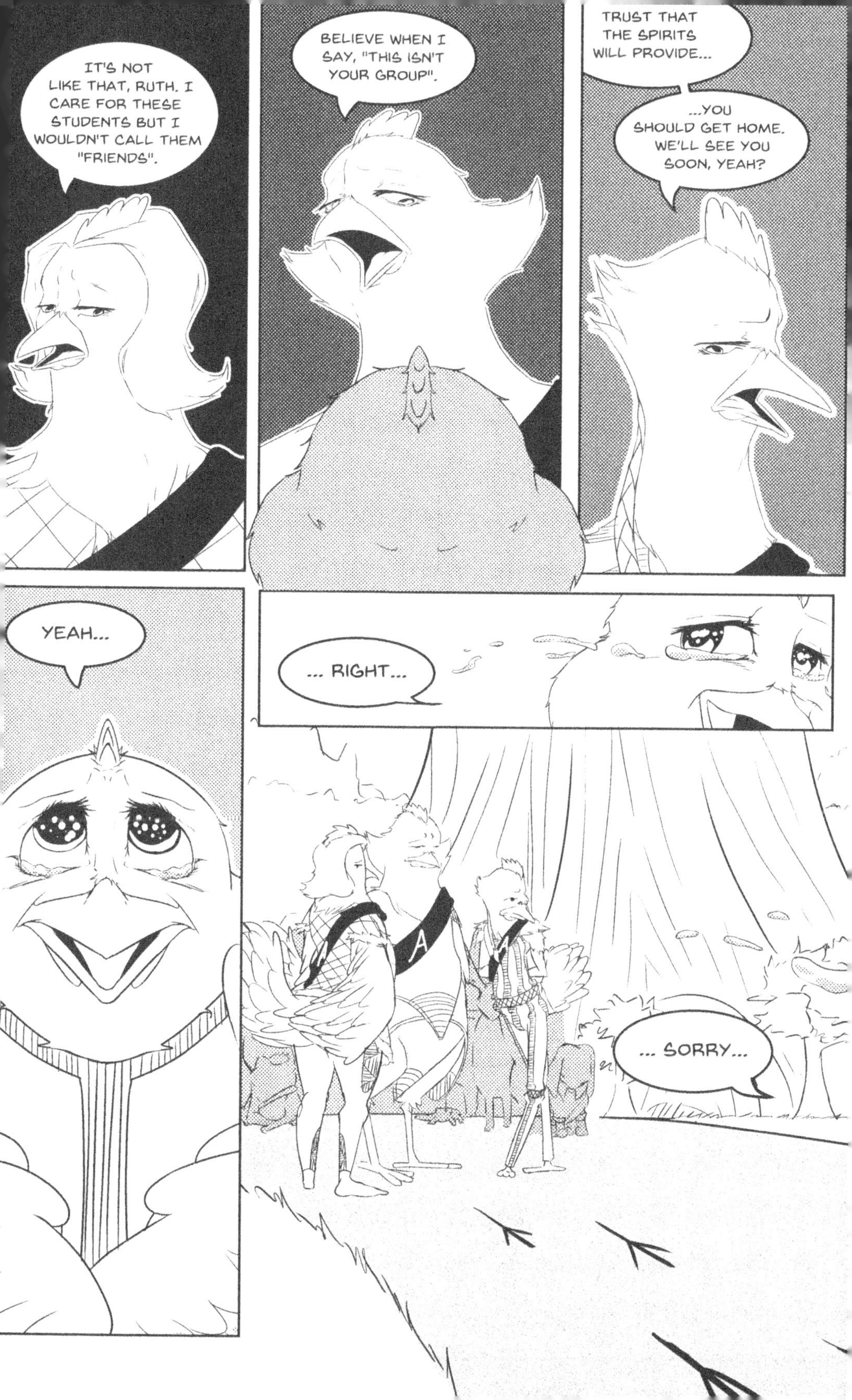
IT'S NOT LIKE THAT, RUTH. I CARE FOR THESE STUDENTS BUT I WOULDN'T CALL THEM "FRIENDS".
BELIEVE WHEN I SAY, "THIS ISN'T YOUR GROUP".
TRUST THAT THE SPIRITS WILL PROVIDE...
...YOU SHOULD GET HOME. WE'LL SEE YOU SOON, YEAH?
YEAH...
... RIGHT...
... SORRY...

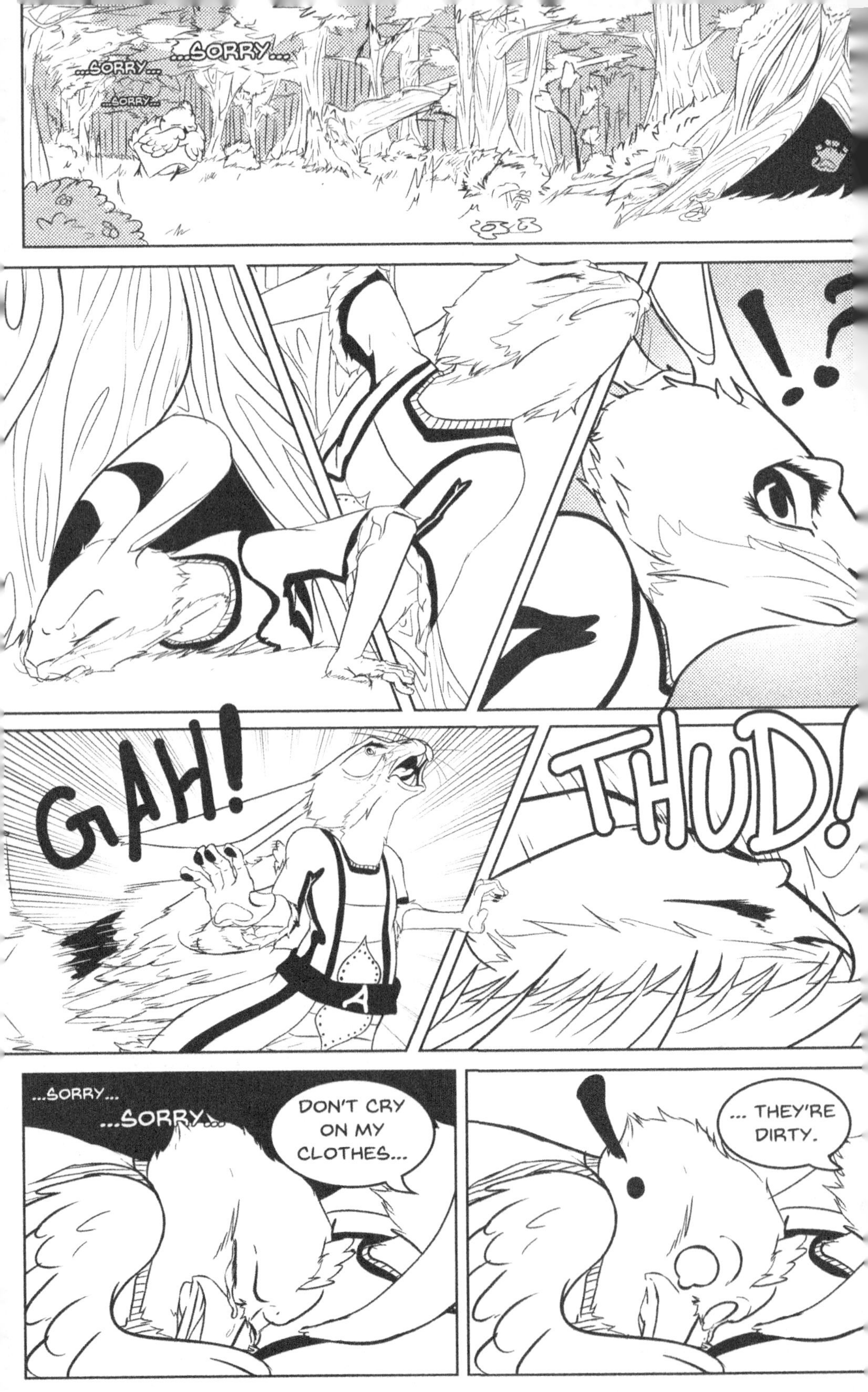

...SORRY...
...SORRY...
...SORRY...
!?
GAH!
THUD!
...SORRY...
...SORRY...
DON'T CRY ON MY CLOTHES...
!
... THEY'RE DIRTY.

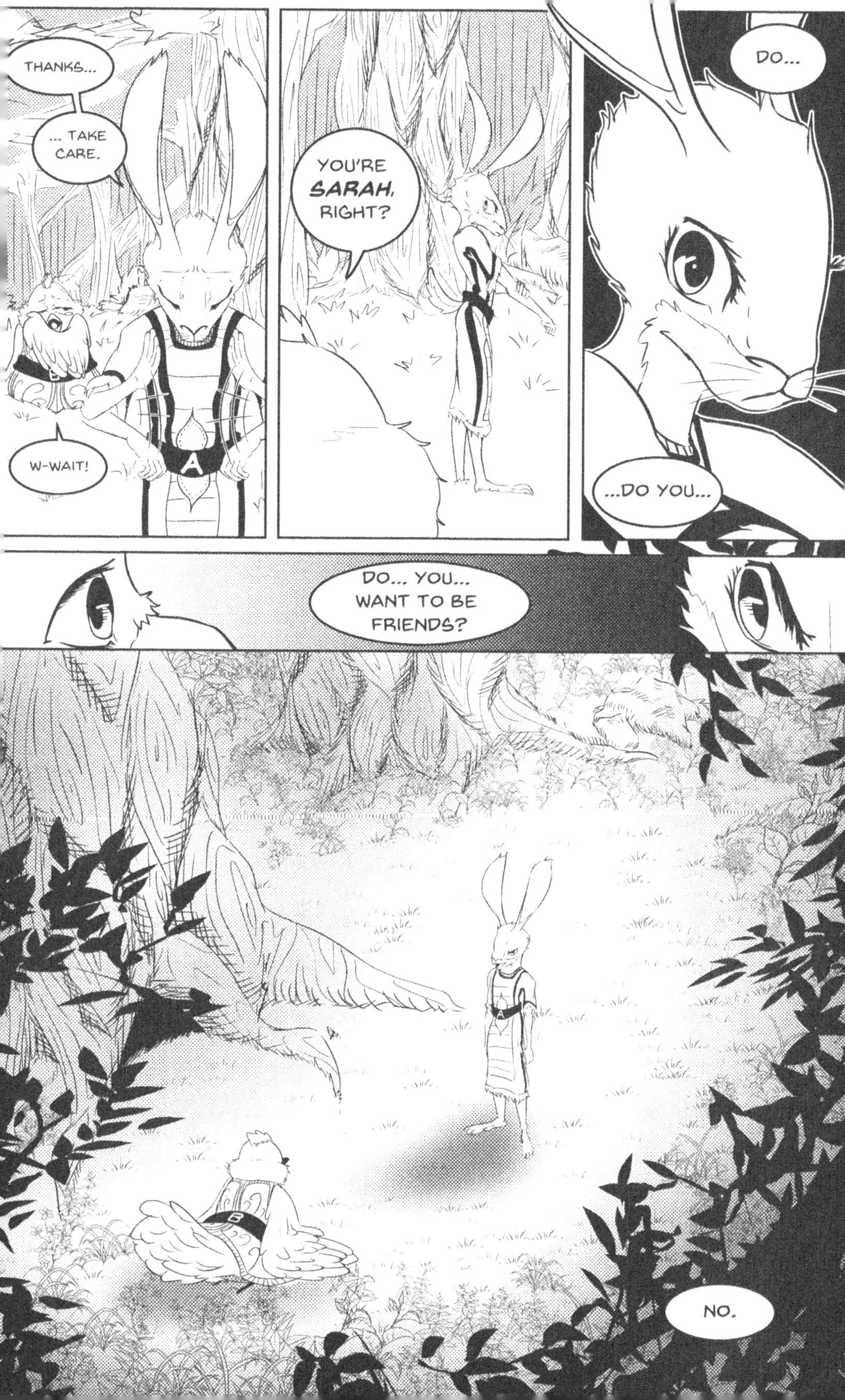
THANKS...
... TAKE CARE.
W-WAIT!
YOU'RE SARAH, RIGHT?
DO...
...DO YOU...
DO... YOU... WANT TO BE FRIENDS?
NO.

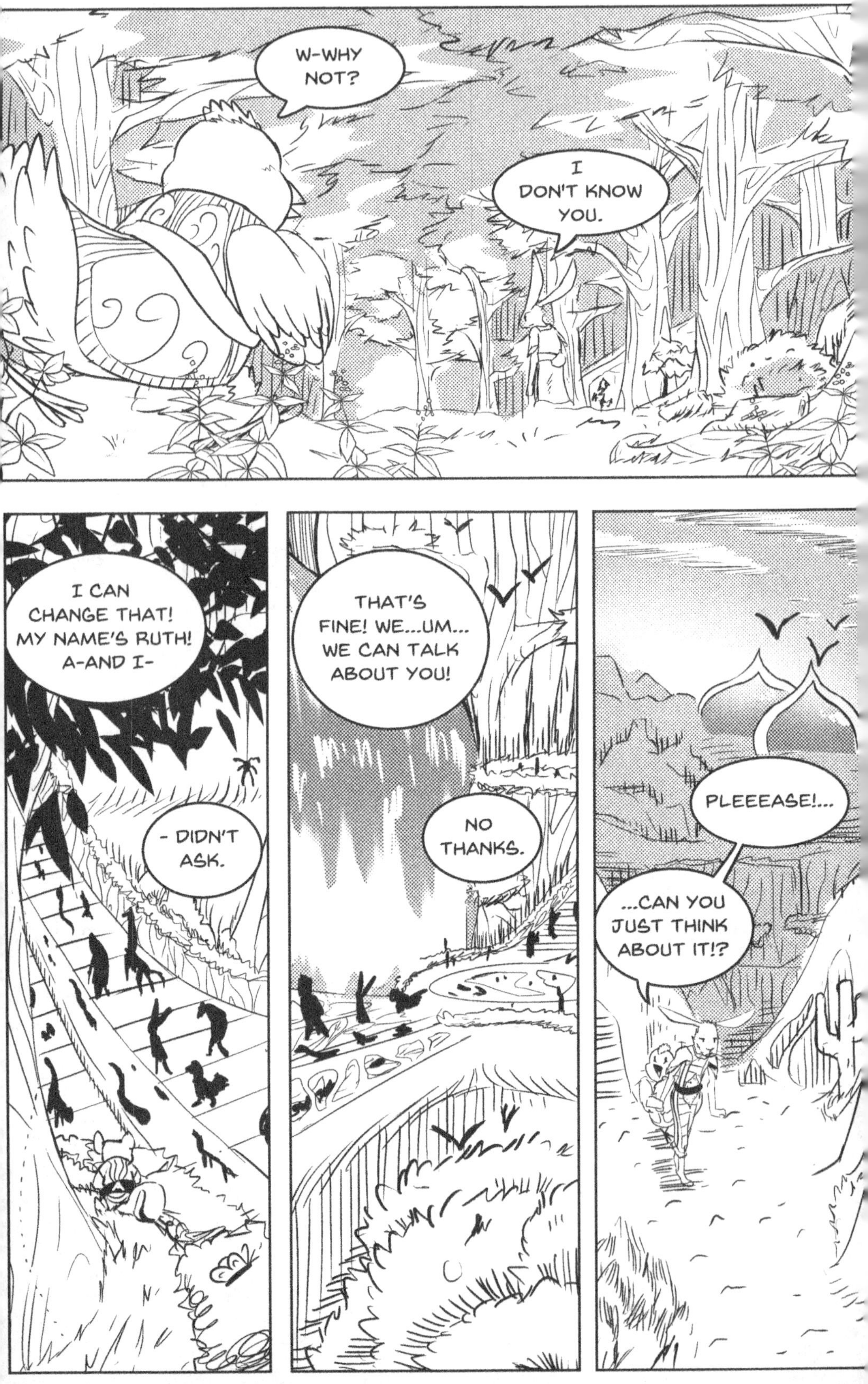
W-WHY NOT?
I DON'T KNOW YOU.
I CAN CHANGE THAT! MY NAME'S RUTH! A-AND I-
- DIDN'T ASK.
THAT'S FINE! WE...UM... WE CAN TALK ABOUT YOU!
NO THANKS.
PLEEEASE!...
...CAN YOU JUST THINK ABOUT IT!?

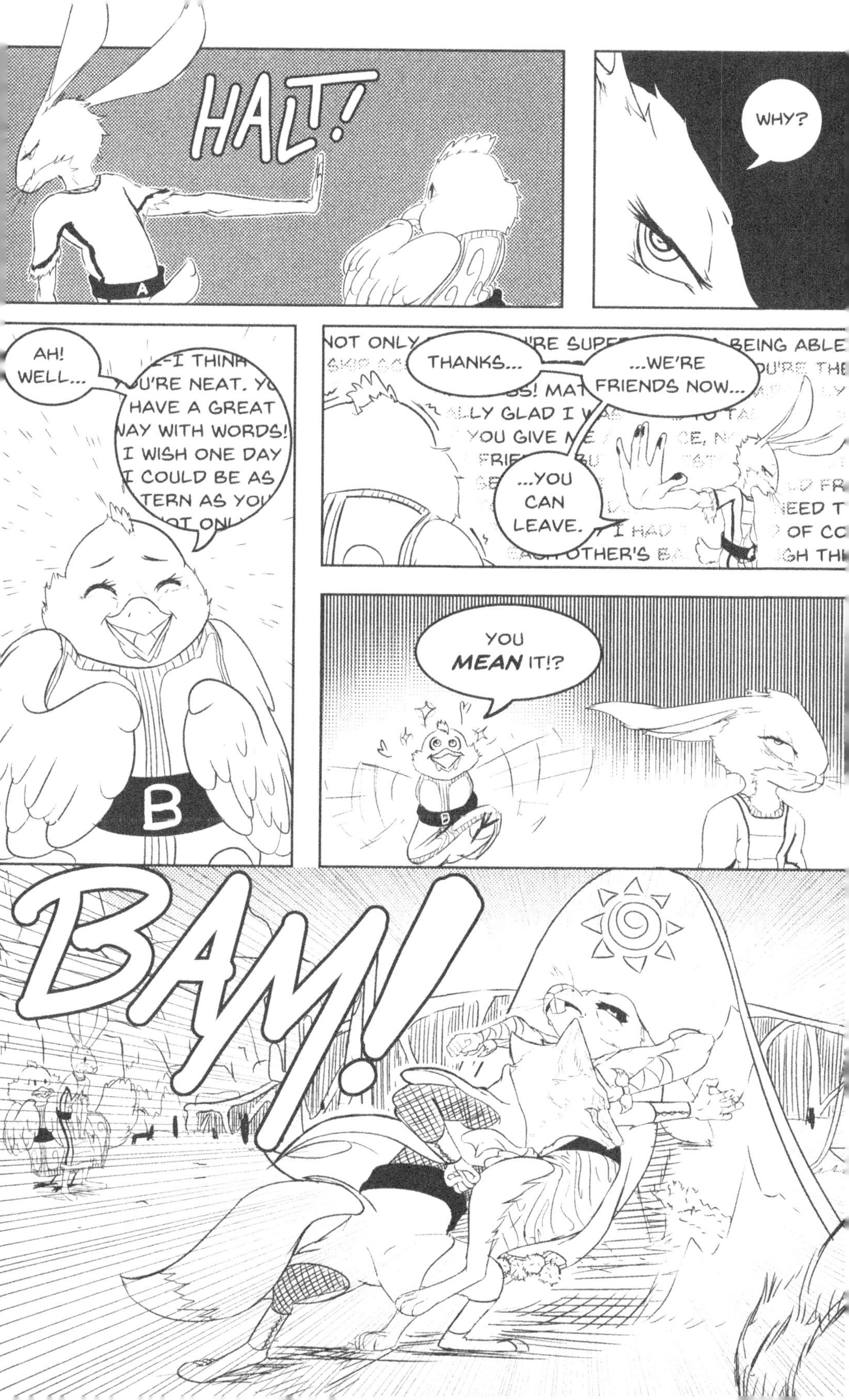
HALT!
WHY?
AH! WELL...
I THINK YOU'RE NEAT. YOU HAVE A GREAT WAY WITH WORDS! I WISH ONE DAY I COULD BE AS STERN AS YOU
THANKS...
...WE'RE FRIENDS NOW...
...YOU CAN LEAVE.
YOU MEAN IT!?
BAM!

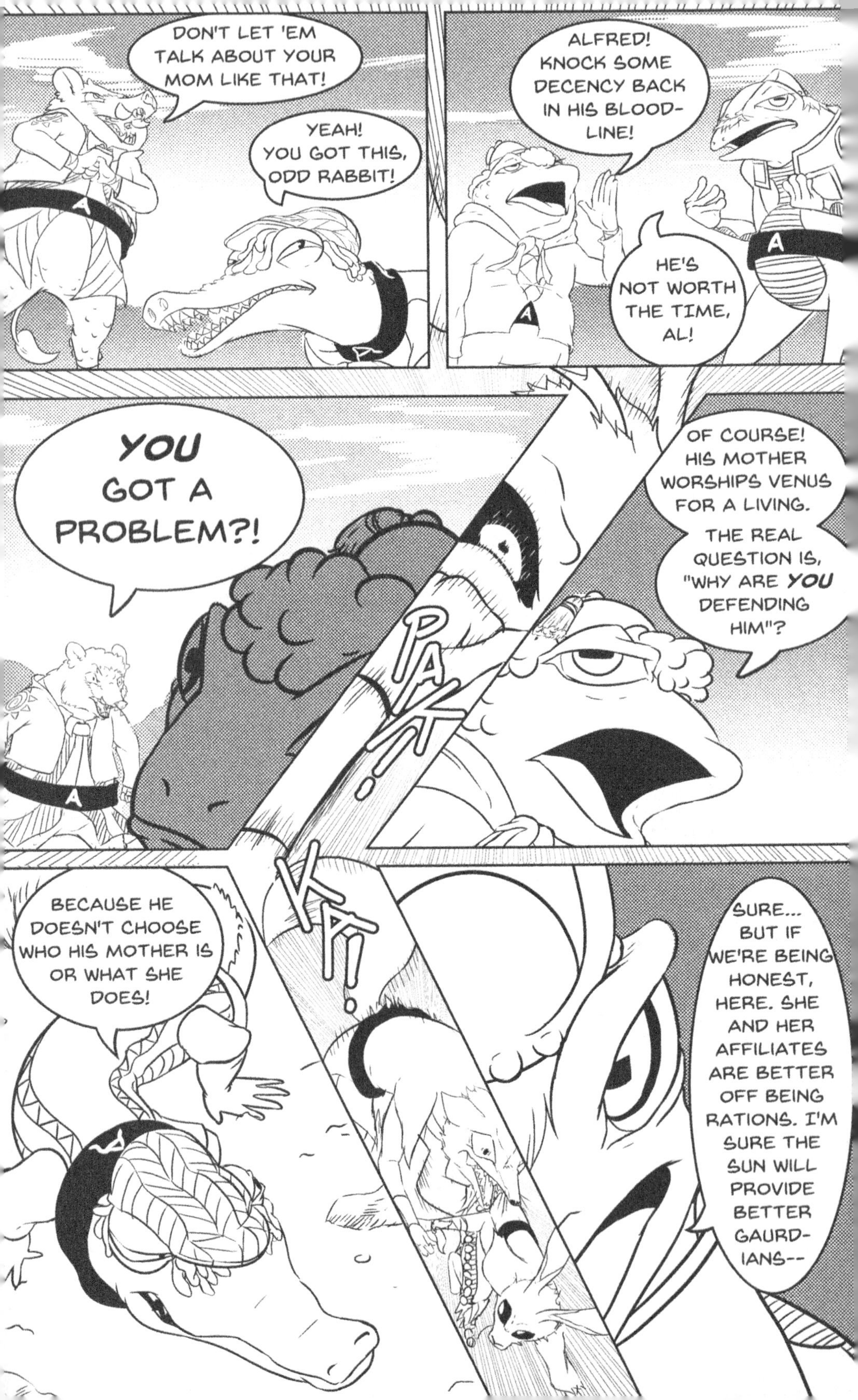
DON'T LET 'EM TALK ABOUT YOUR MOM LIKE THAT!
YEAH! YOU GOT THIS, ODD RABBIT!
ALFRED! KNOCK SOME DECENCY BACK IN HIS BLOOD-LINE!
HE'S NOT WORTH THE TIME, AL!
YOU GOT A PROBLEM?!
PAK!
OF COURSE! HIS MOTHER WORSHIPS VENUS FOR A LIVING.
THE REAL QUESTION IS, "WHY ARE YOU DEFENDING HIM"?
KA!
BECAUSE HE DOESN'T CHOOSE WHO HIS MOTHER IS OR WHAT SHE DOES!
SURE... BUT IF WE'RE BEING HONEST, HERE. SHE AND HER AFFILIATES ARE BETTER OFF BEING RATIONS. I'M SURE THE SUN WILL PROVIDE BETTER GAURD-IANS--

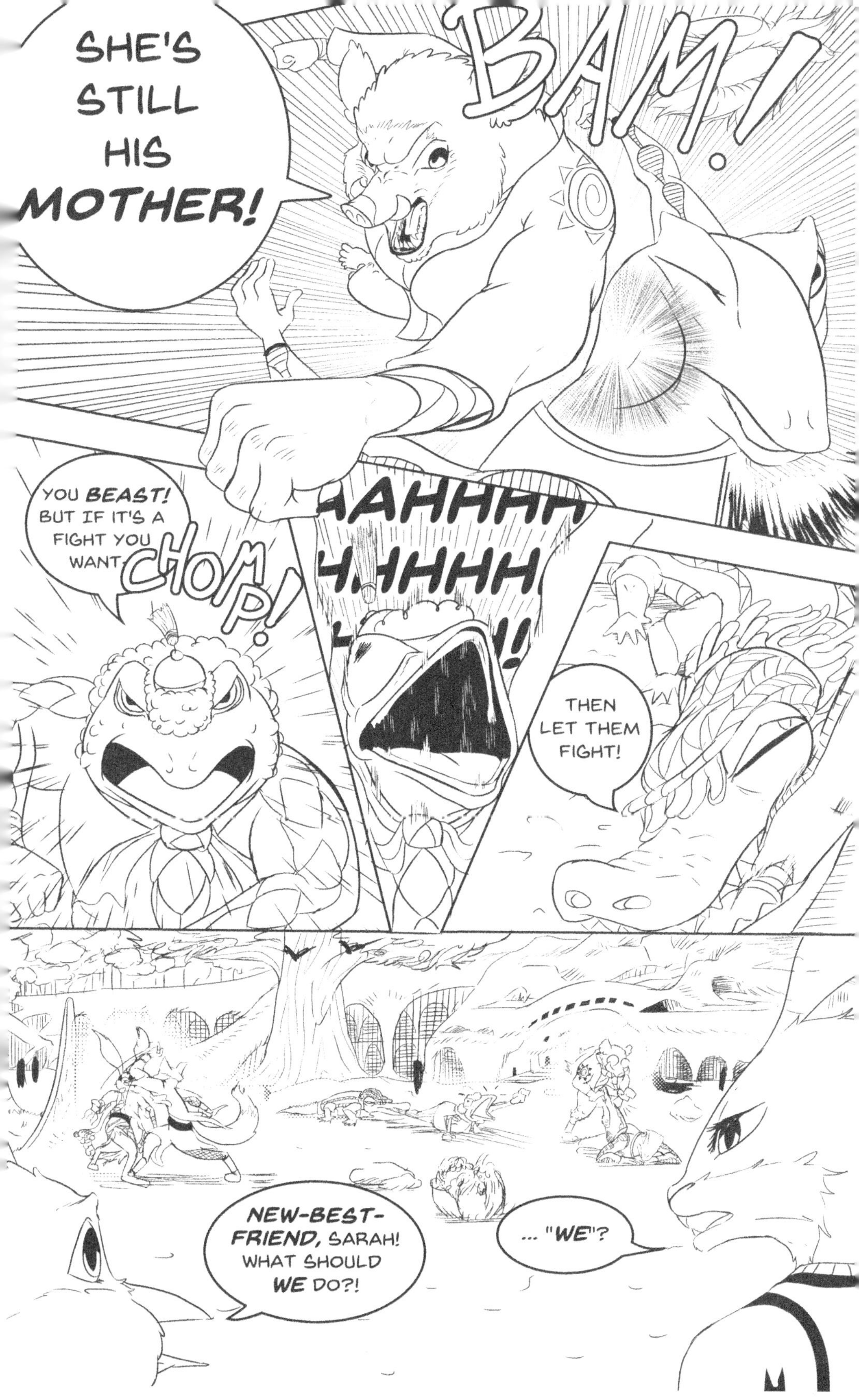
SHE'S STILL HIS MOTHER!
BAM!
YOU BEAST! BUT IF IT'S A FIGHT YOU WANT-
CHOMP!
AAHHHH HHHHH
THEN LET THEM FIGHT!
NEW-BEST-FRIEND, SARAH! WHAT SHOULD WE DO?!
... "WE"?

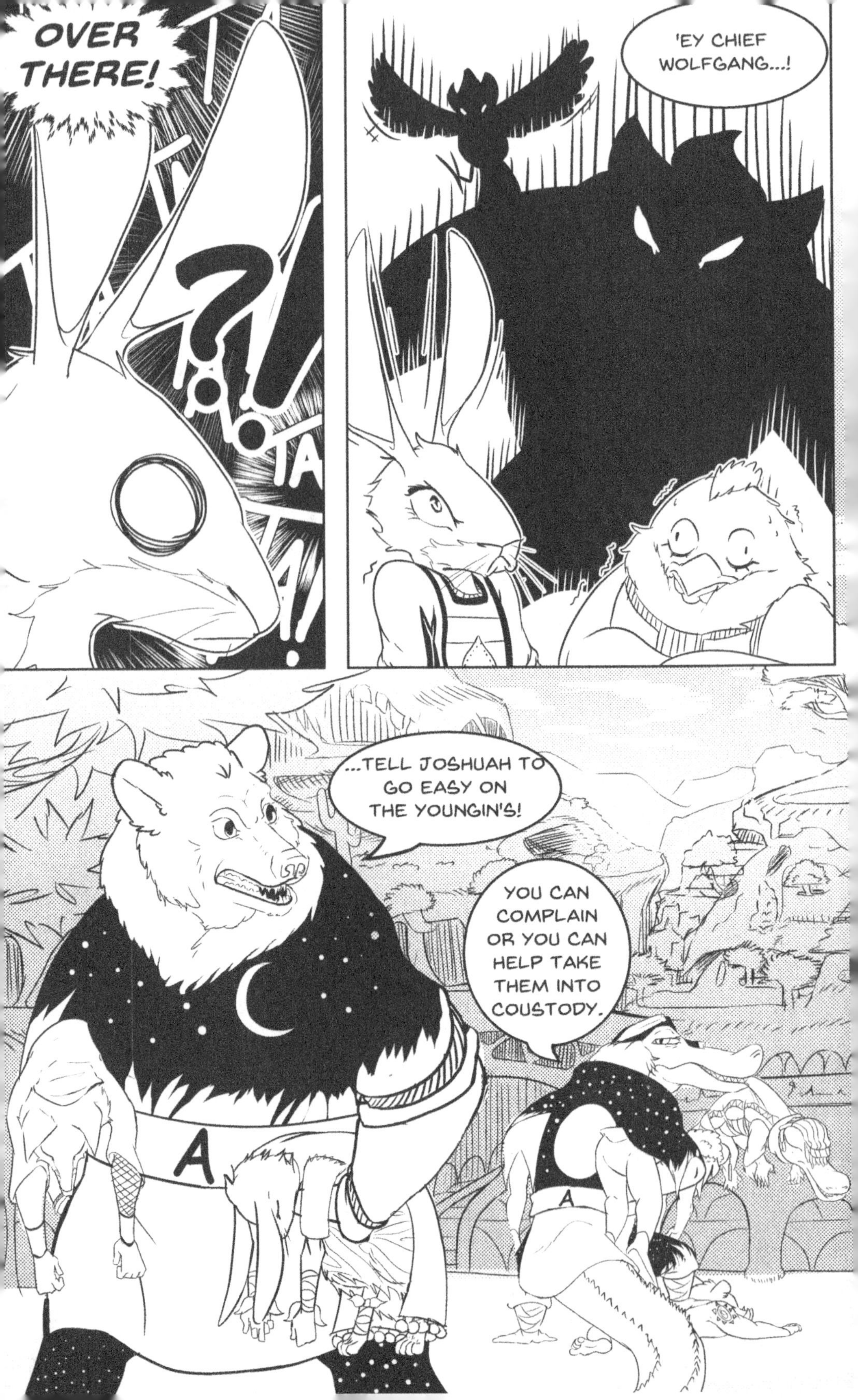
OVER THERE!
'EY CHIEF WOLFGANG...!
...TELL JOSHUAH TO GO EASY ON THE YOUNGIN'S!
YOU CAN COMPLAIN OR YOU CAN HELP TAKE THEM INTO COUSTODY.

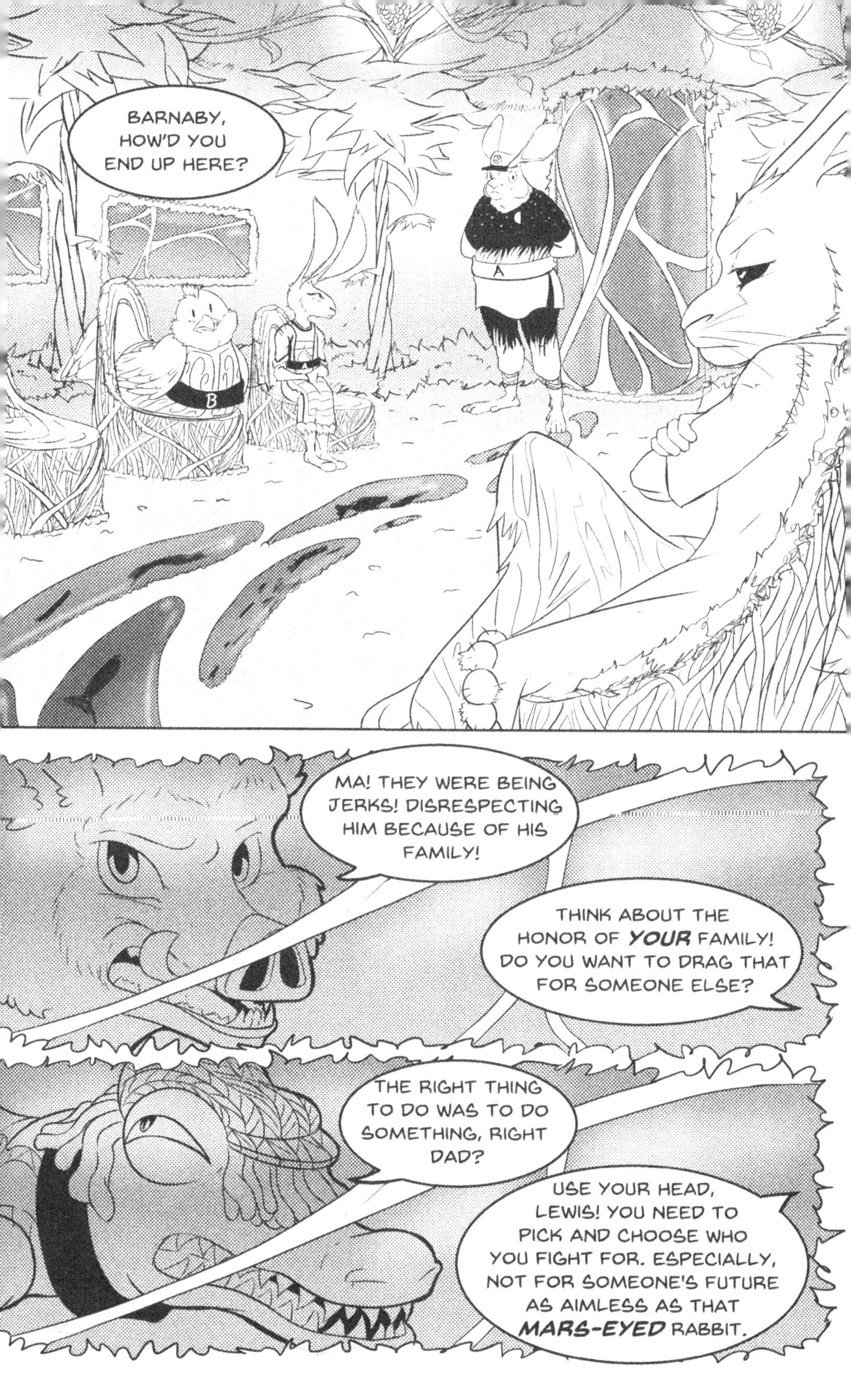
BARNABY, HOW'D YOU END UP HERE?
MA! THEY WERE BEING JERKS! DISRESPECTING HIM BECAUSE OF HIS FAMILY!
THINK ABOUT THE HONOR OF **YOUR** FAMILY! DO YOU WANT TO DRAG THAT FOR SOMEONE ELSE?
THE RIGHT THING TO DO WAS TO DO SOMETHING, RIGHT DAD?
USE YOUR HEAD, LEWIS! YOU NEED TO PICK AND CHOOSE WHO YOU FIGHT FOR. ESPECIALLY, NOT FOR SOMEONE'S FUTURE AS AIMLESS AS THAT **MARS-EYED** RABBIT.

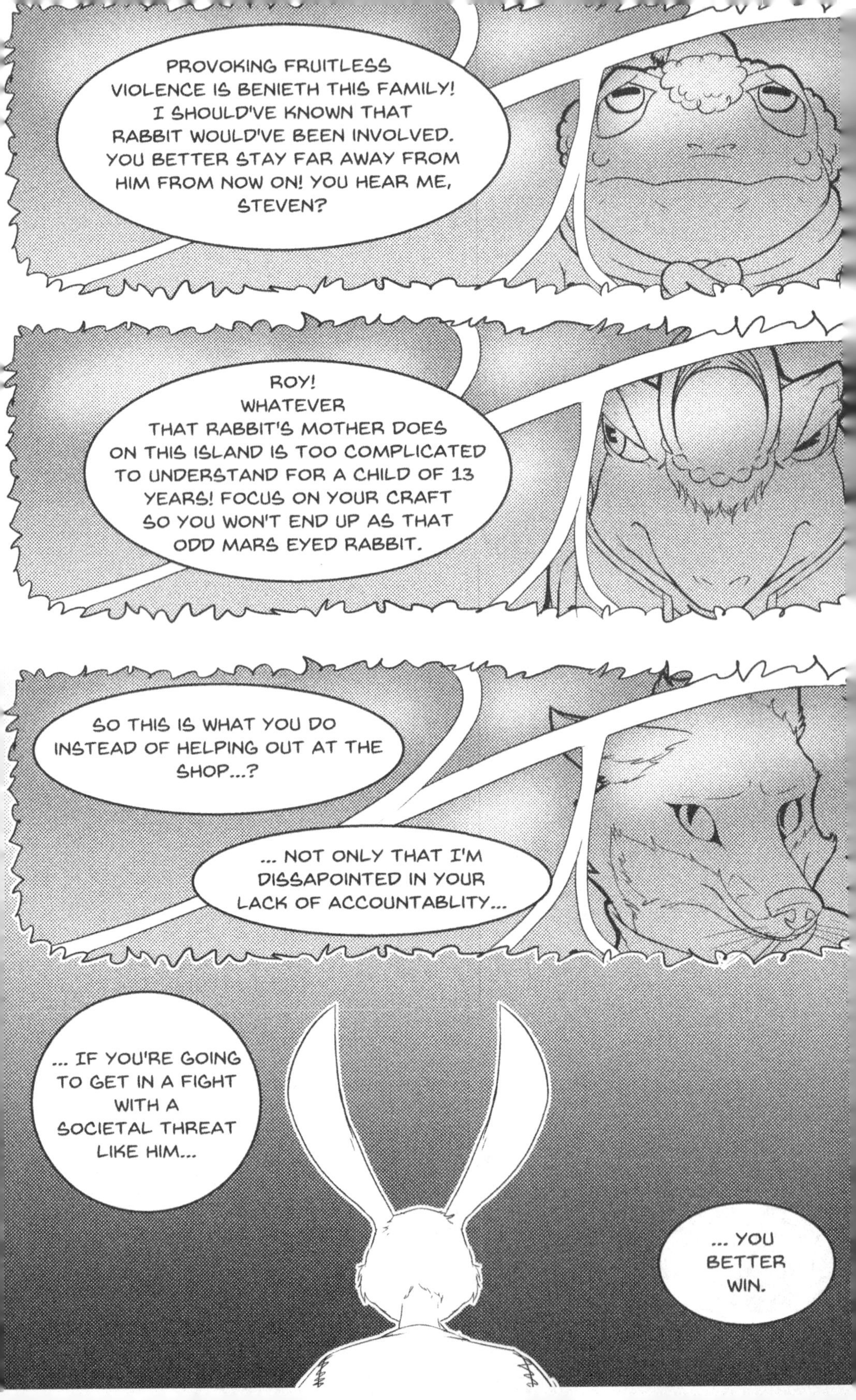
PROVOKING FRUITLESS VIOLENCE IS BENIETH THIS FAMILY! I SHOULD'VE KNOWN THAT RABBIT WOULD'VE BEEN INVOLVED. YOU BETTER STAY FAR AWAY FROM HIM FROM NOW ON! YOU HEAR ME, STEVEN?
ROY! WHATEVER THAT RABBIT'S MOTHER DOES ON THIS ISLAND IS TOO COMPLICATED TO UNDERSTAND FOR A CHILD OF 13 YEARS! FOCUS ON YOUR CRAFT SO YOU WON'T END UP AS THAT ODD MARS EYED RABBIT.
SO THIS IS WHAT YOU DO INSTEAD OF HELPING OUT AT THE SHOP...?
... NOT ONLY THAT I'M DISSAPOINTED IN YOUR LACK OF ACCOUNTABLITY...
... IF YOU'RE GOING TO GET IN A FIGHT WITH A SOCIETAL THREAT LIKE HIM...
... YOU BETTER WIN.

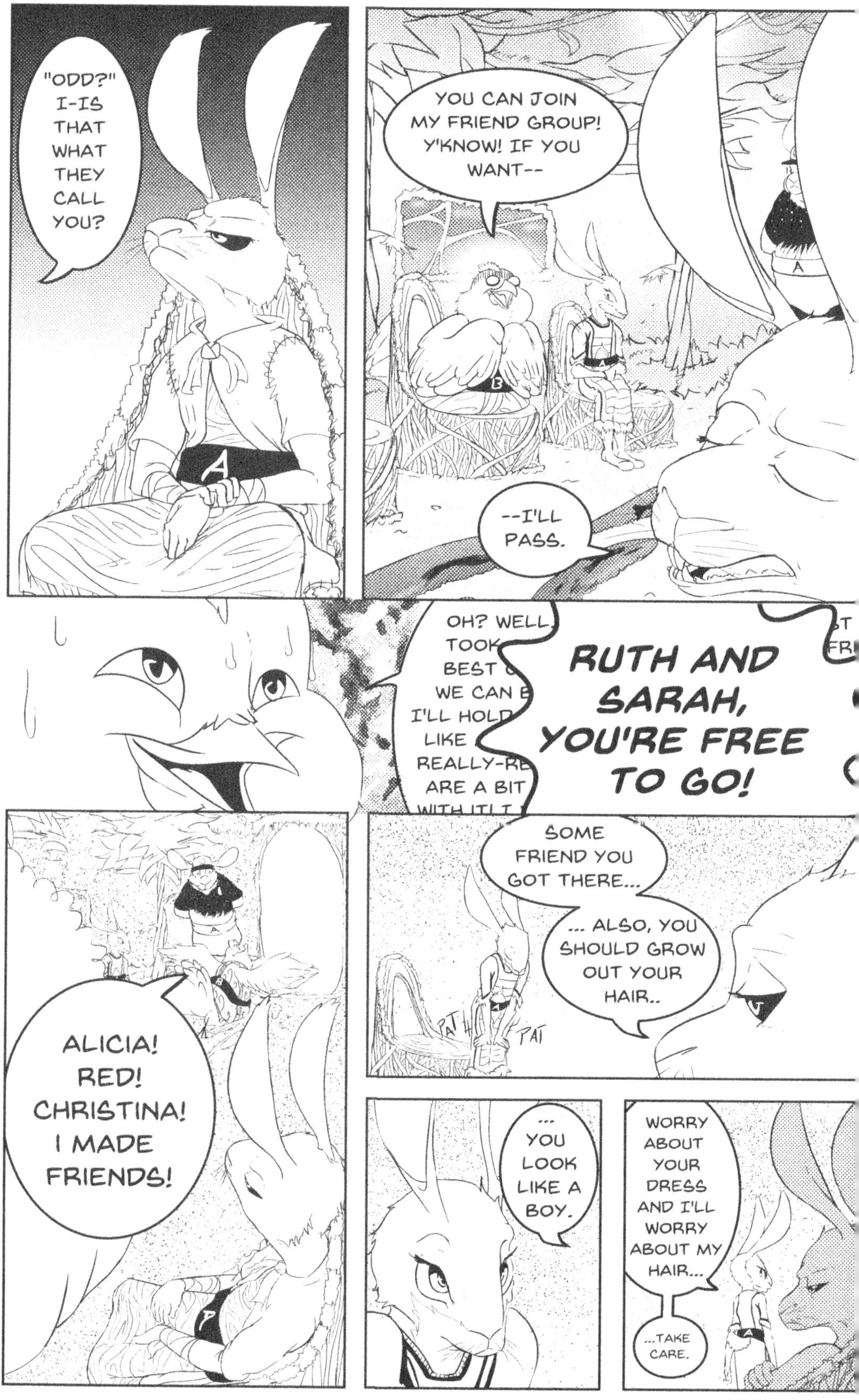
"ODD?" I-IS THAT WHAT THEY CALL YOU?
YOU CAN JOIN MY FRIEND GROUP! Y'KNOW! IF YOU WANT--
--I'LL PASS.
OH? WELL,
TOOK
BEST
WE CAN
I'LL HOLD
LIKE
ARE A BIT
WITH IT!
RUTH AND SARAH, YOU'RE FREE TO GO!
ALICIA! RED! CHRISTINA! I MADE FRIENDS!
SOME FRIEND YOU GOT THERE...
... ALSO, YOU SHOULD GROW OUT YOUR HAIR..
PAT
PAT
... YOU LOOK LIKE A BOY.
WORRY ABOUT YOUR DRESS AND I'LL WORRY ABOUT MY HAIR...
...TAKE CARE.

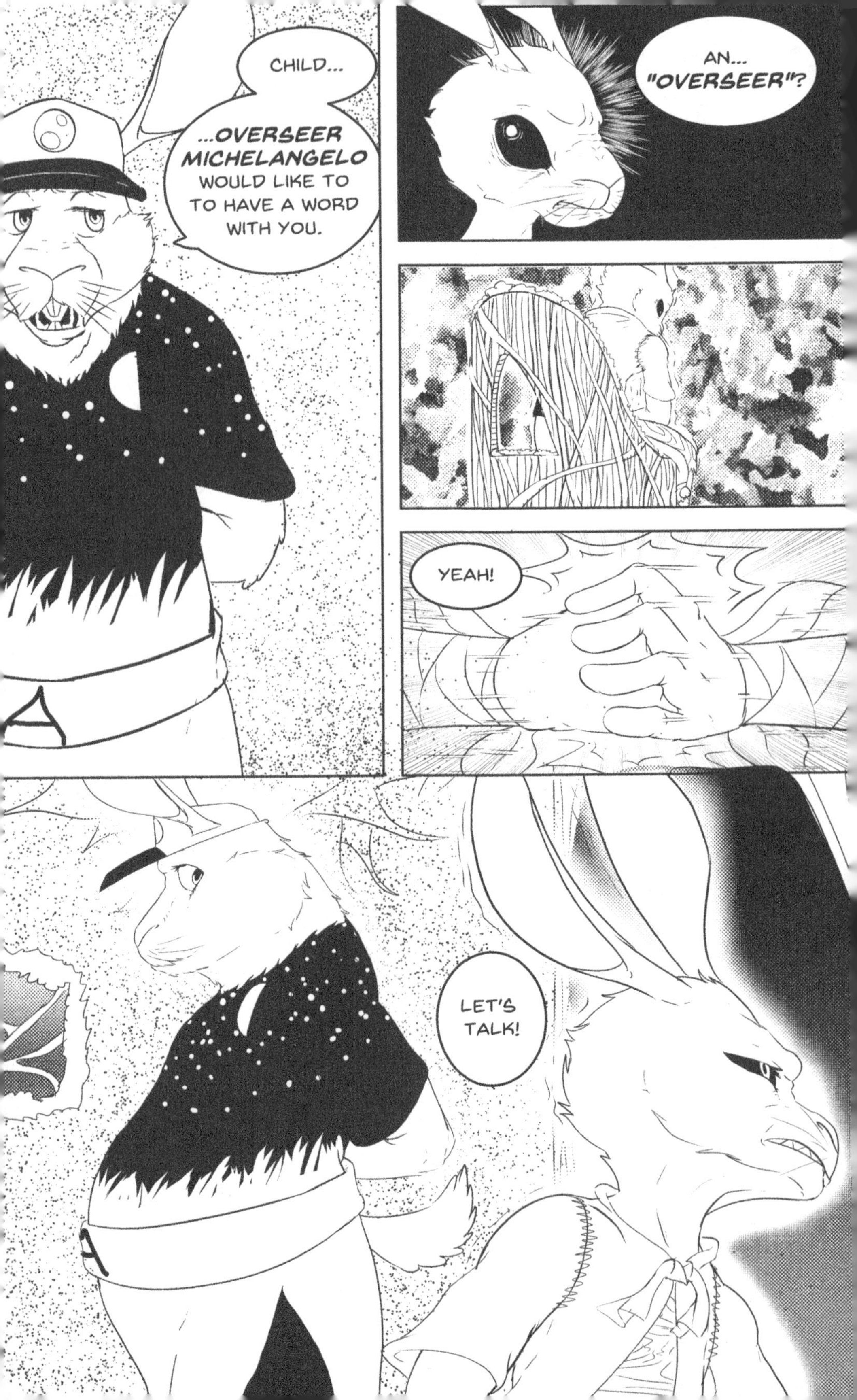
CHILD...
...OVERSEER MICHELANGELO WOULD LIKE TO TO HAVE A WORD WITH YOU.
AN... "OVERSEER"?
YEAH!
LET'S TALK!

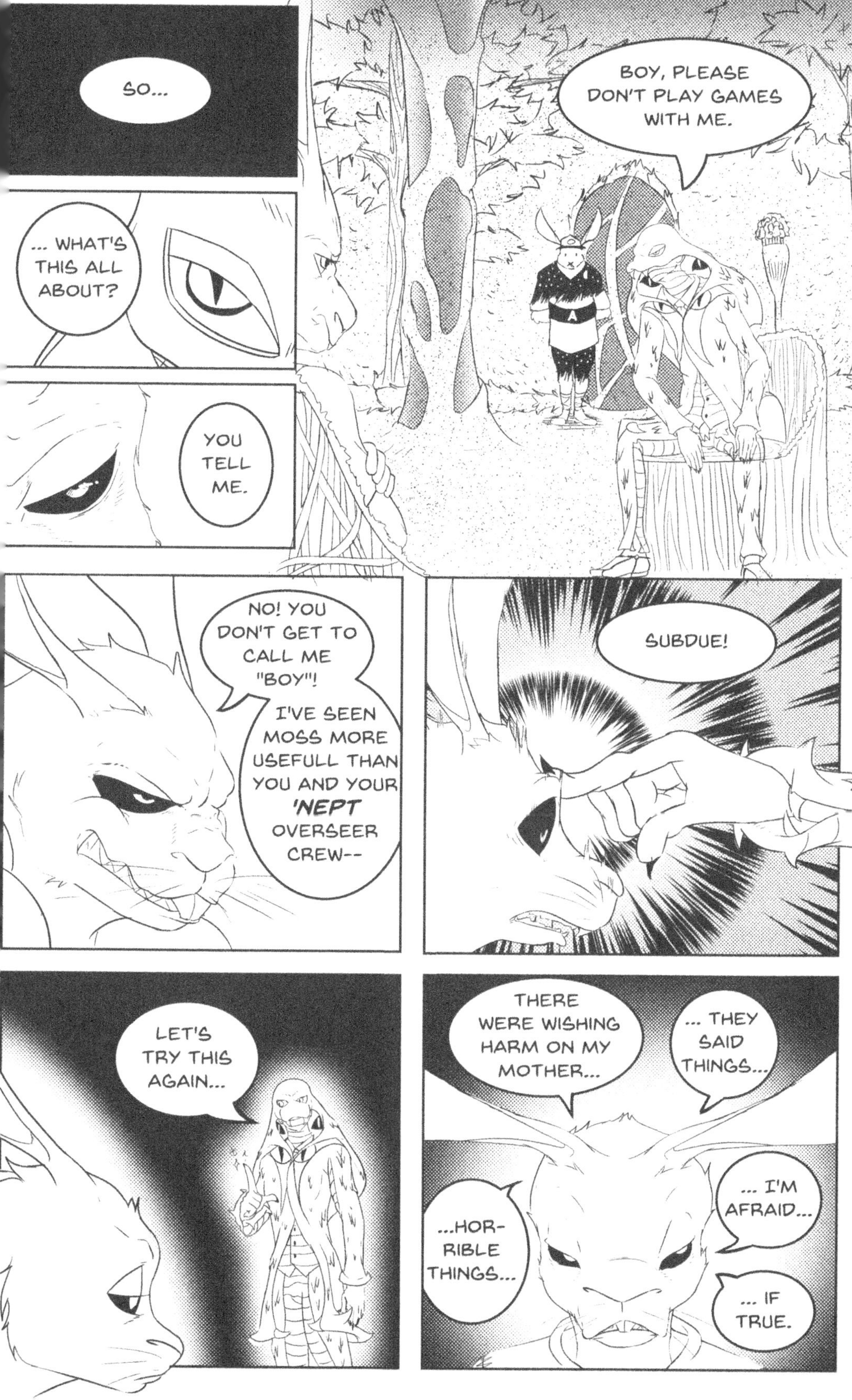
SO...
... WHAT'S THIS ALL ABOUT?
YOU TELL ME.
BOY, PLEASE DON'T PLAY GAMES WITH ME.
NO! YOU DON'T GET TO CALL ME "BOY"!
I'VE SEEN MOSS MORE USEFULL THAN YOU AND YOUR 'NEPT OVERSEER CREW--
SUBDUE!
LET'S TRY THIS AGAIN...
THERE WERE WISHING HARM ON MY MOTHER...
... THEY SAID THINGS...
...HOR-RIBLE THINGS...
... I'M AFRAID...
... IF TRUE.

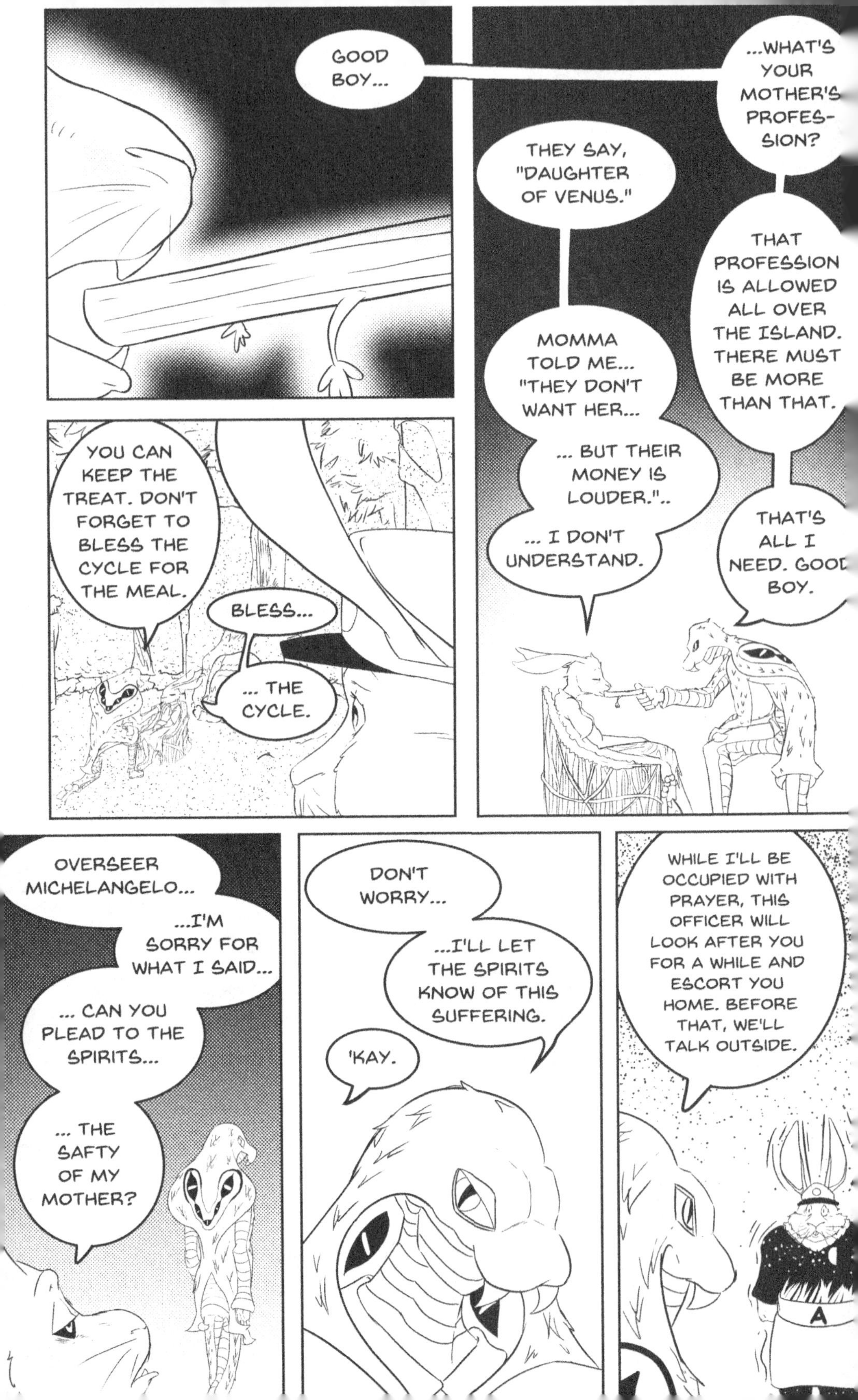
GOOD BOY...
YOU CAN KEEP THE TREAT. DON'T FORGET TO BLESS THE CYCLE FOR THE MEAL.
BLESS...
... THE CYCLE.
...WHAT'S YOUR MOTHER'S PROFES-SION?
THEY SAY, "DAUGHTER OF VENUS."
THAT PROFESSION IS ALLOWED ALL OVER THE ISLAND. THERE MUST BE MORE THAN THAT.
MOMMA TOLD ME... "THEY DON'T WANT HER...
... BUT THEIR MONEY IS LOUDER."..
... I DON'T UNDERSTAND.
THAT'S ALL I NEED. GOOD BOY.
OVERSEER MICHELANGELO...
...I'M SORRY FOR WHAT I SAID...
... CAN YOU PLEAD TO THE SPIRITS...
... THE SAFTY OF MY MOTHER?
DON'T WORRY...
...I'LL LET THE SPIRITS KNOW OF THIS SUFFERING.
'KAY.
WHILE I'LL BE OCCUPIED WITH PRAYER, THIS OFFICER WILL LOOK AFTER YOU FOR A WHILE AND ESCORT YOU HOME. BEFORE THAT, WE'LL TALK OUTSIDE.
A

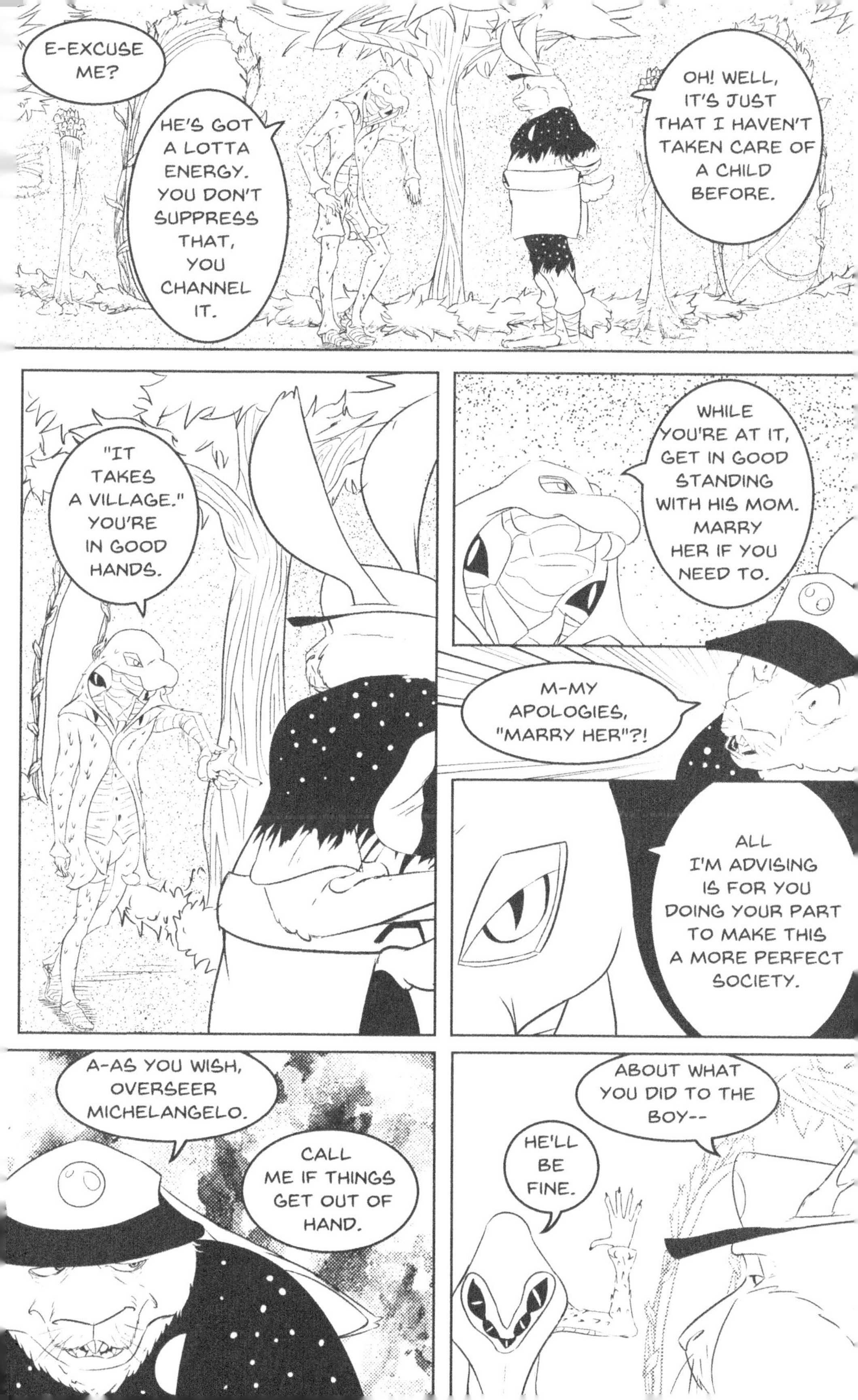
E-EXCUSE ME?
HE'S GOT A LOTTA ENERGY. YOU DON'T SUPPRESS THAT, YOU CHANNEL IT.
OH! WELL, IT'S JUST THAT I HAVEN'T TAKEN CARE OF A CHILD BEFORE.
"IT TAKES A VILLAGE." YOU'RE IN GOOD HANDS.
WHILE YOU'RE AT IT, GET IN GOOD STANDING WITH HIS MOM. MARRY HER IF YOU NEED TO.
M-MY APOLOGIES, "MARRY HER"?!
ALL I'M ADVISING IS FOR YOU DOING YOUR PART TO MAKE THIS A MORE PERFECT SOCIETY.
A-AS YOU WISH, OVERSEER MICHELANGELO.
CALL ME IF THINGS GET OUT OF HAND.
ABOUT WHAT YOU DID TO THE BOY--
HE'LL BE FINE.

ALRIGHT, FIONA. LET'S GO HOME

ARE WE GOING TO DO SOMETHING ABOUT THE RABBIT GIRL?

A

THAT'S TOMORROW'S PROBLEM...

...WHEN I HEARD IT WAS FIELD CHIMERA'S CHILD GETTING INTO TROUBLE, IT SOUNDED LIKE A PROBLEM THAT'S BEEN BREWING FOR LONG ENOUGH.

FAIR ENOUGH, I'M JUST AFRAID SHE MIGHT HAVE ACCESS TO TOPSIDE.

I'LL FIND A HANDLER TO MAKE SURE SHE'S IN LINE.

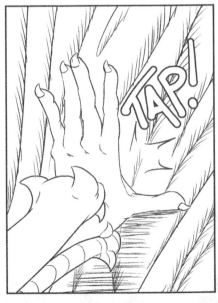

TAP!

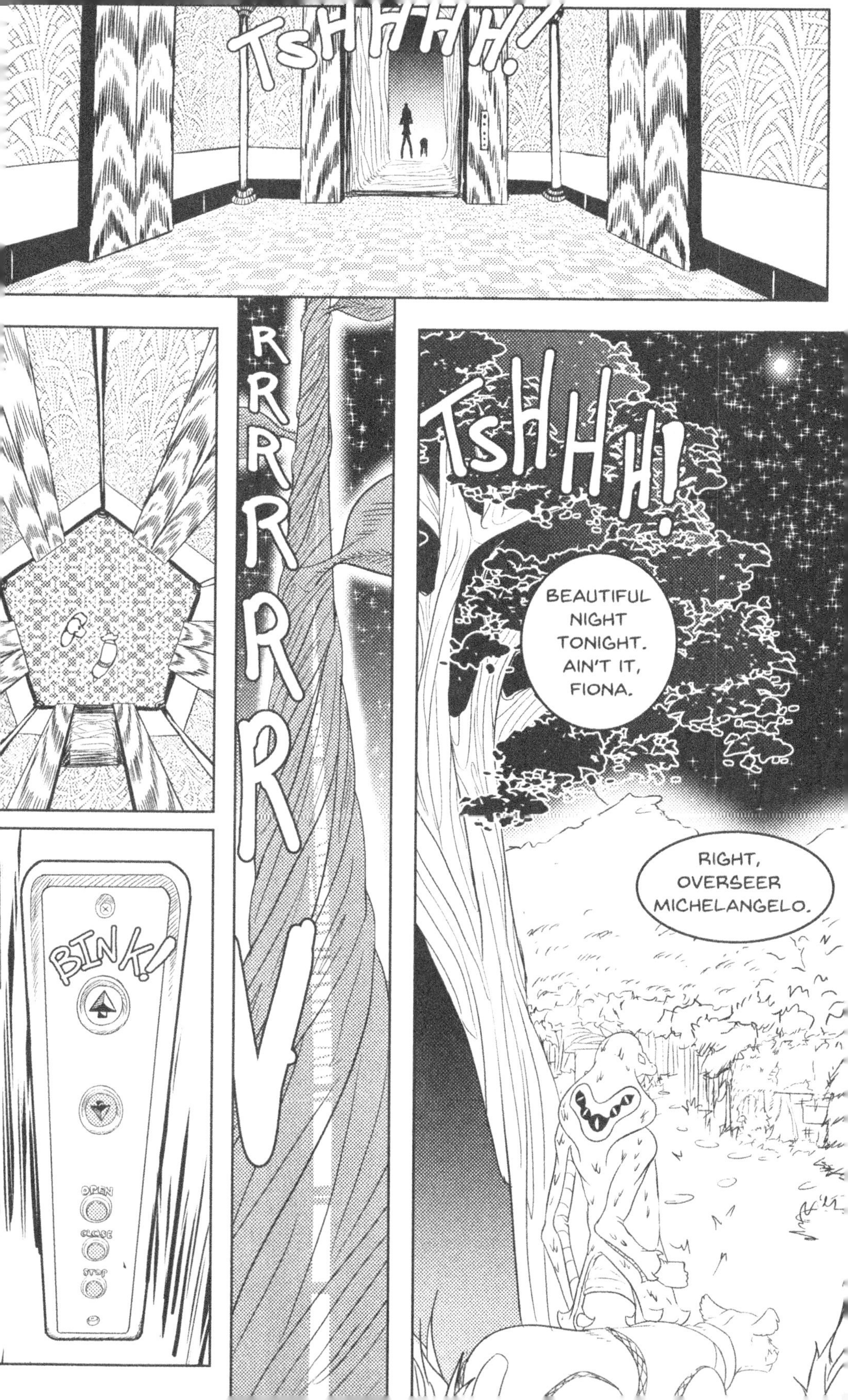
TSHHHHH!
BINK!
OPEN
CLOSE
STOP
RRRRRRR
TSHHH!
BEAUTIFUL NIGHT TONIGHT. AIN'T IT, FIONA.
RIGHT, OVERSEER MICHELANGELO.

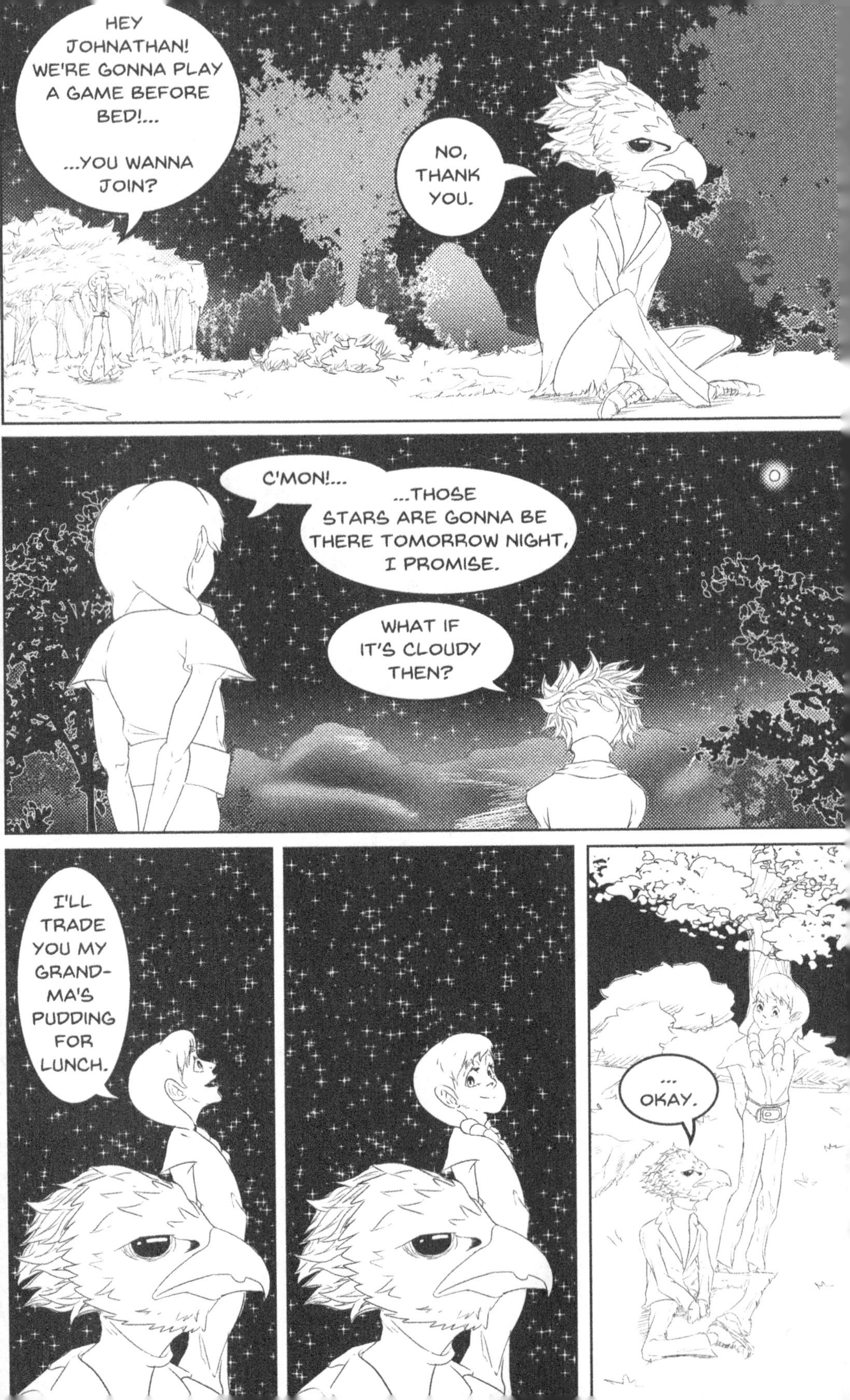
HEY JOHNATHAN! WE'RE GONNA PLAY A GAME BEFORE BED!... ...YOU WANNA JOIN?
NO, THANK YOU.
C'MON!...
...THOSE STARS ARE GONNA BE THERE TOMORROW NIGHT, I PROMISE.
WHAT IF IT'S CLOUDY THEN?
I'LL TRADE YOU MY GRAND-MA'S PUDDING FOR LUNCH.
... OKAY.

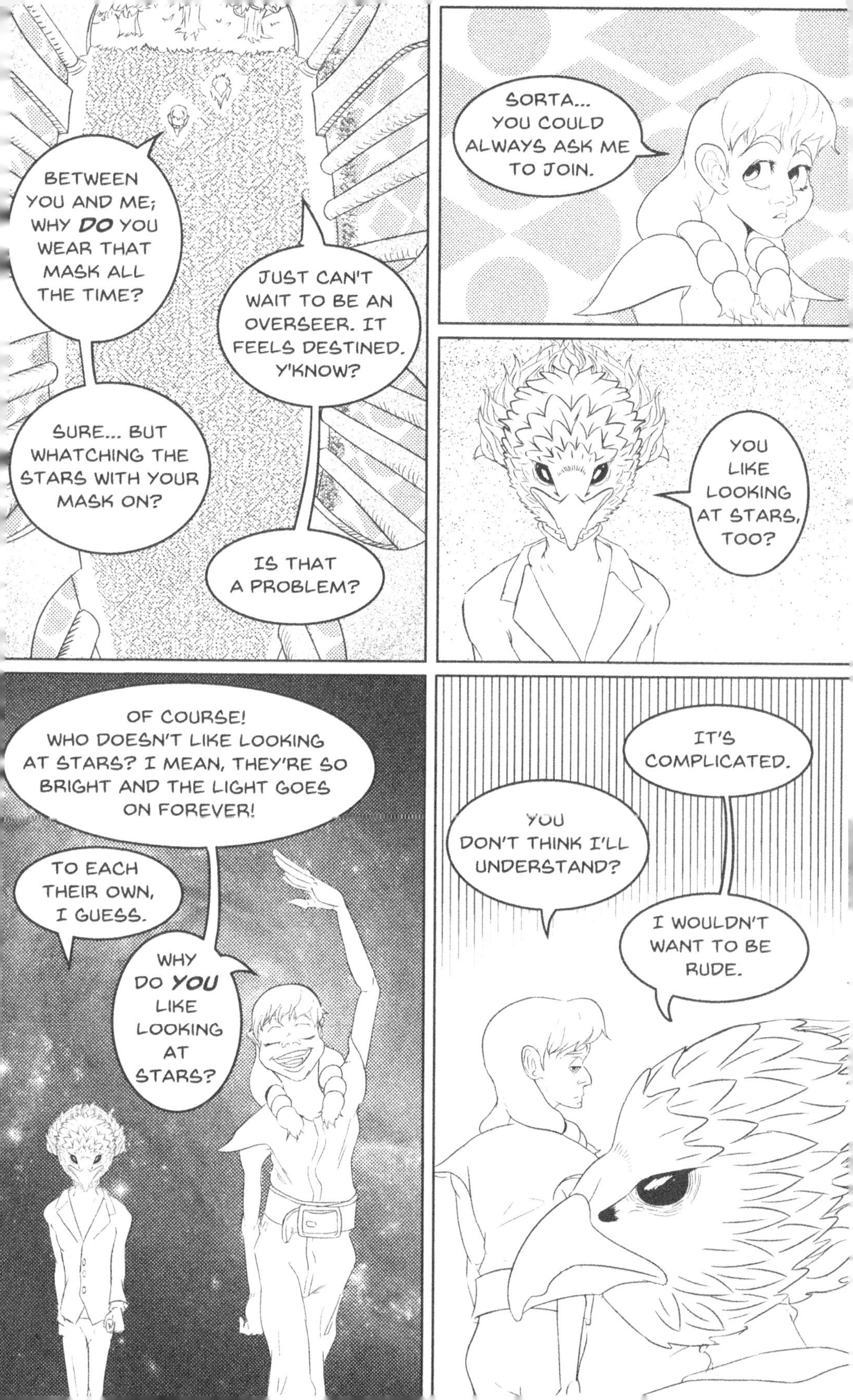
BETWEEN YOU AND ME; WHY DO YOU WEAR THAT MASK ALL THE TIME?
JUST CAN'T WAIT TO BE AN OVERSEER. IT FEELS DESTINED. Y'KNOW?
SURE... BUT WHATCHING THE STARS WITH YOUR MASK ON?
IS THAT A PROBLEM?
SORTA... YOU COULD ALWAYS ASK ME TO JOIN.
YOU LIKE LOOKING AT STARS, TOO?
OF COURSE! WHO DOESN'T LIKE LOOKING AT STARS? I MEAN, THEY'RE SO BRIGHT AND THE LIGHT GOES ON FOREVER!
TO EACH THEIR OWN, I GUESS.
WHY DO YOU LIKE LOOKING AT STARS?
IT'S COMPLICATED.
YOU DON'T THINK I'LL UNDERSTAND?
I WOULDN'T WANT TO BE RUDE.

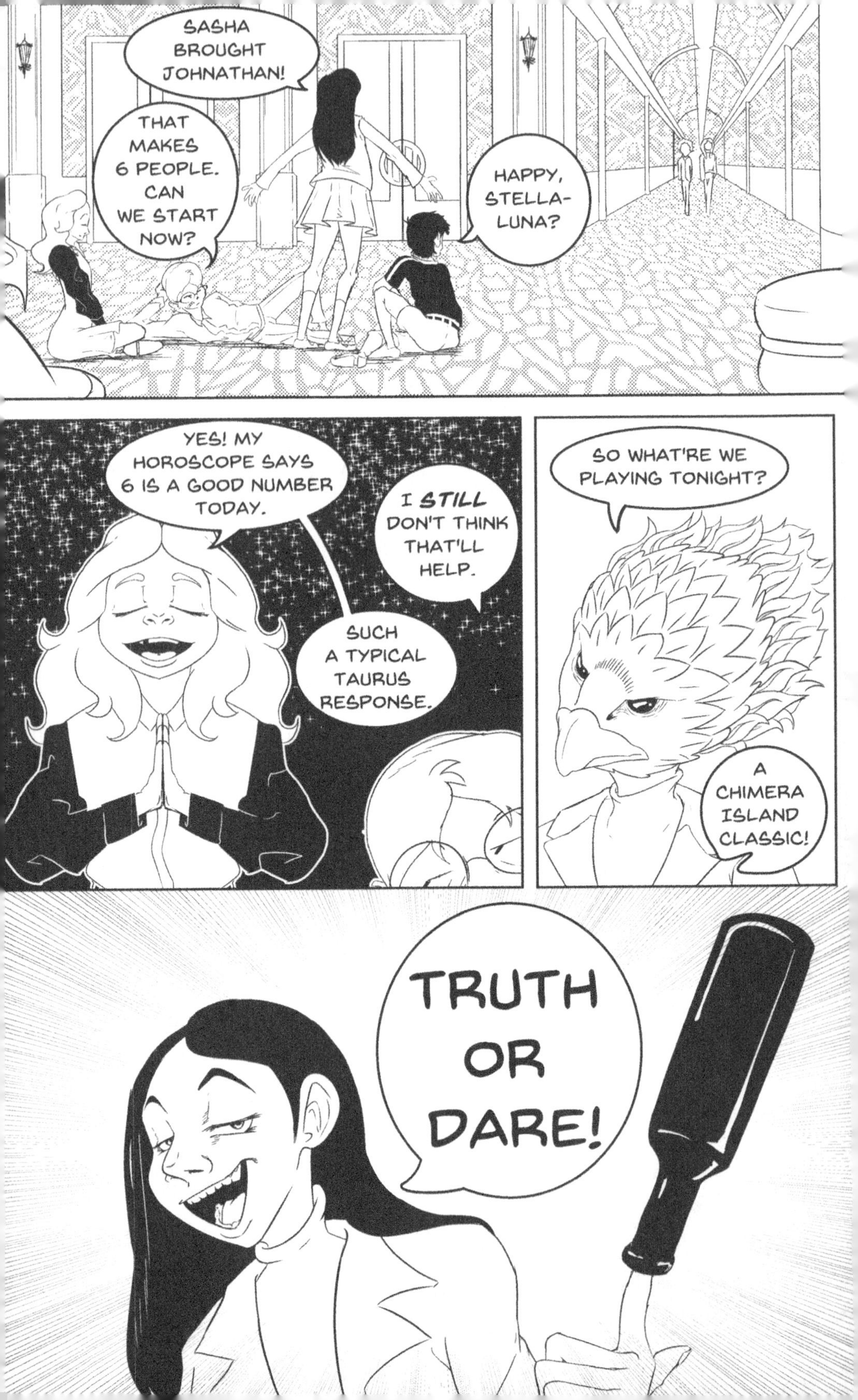
SASHA BROUGHT JOHNATHAN!
THAT MAKES 6 PEOPLE. CAN WE START NOW?
HAPPY, STELLA-LUNA?
YES! MY HOROSCOPE SAYS 6 IS A GOOD NUMBER TODAY.
I *STILL* DON'T THINK THAT'LL HELP.
SUCH A TYPICAL TAURUS RESPONSE.
SO WHAT'RE WE PLAYING TONIGHT?
A CHIMERA ISLAND CLASSIC!
TRUTH OR DARE!

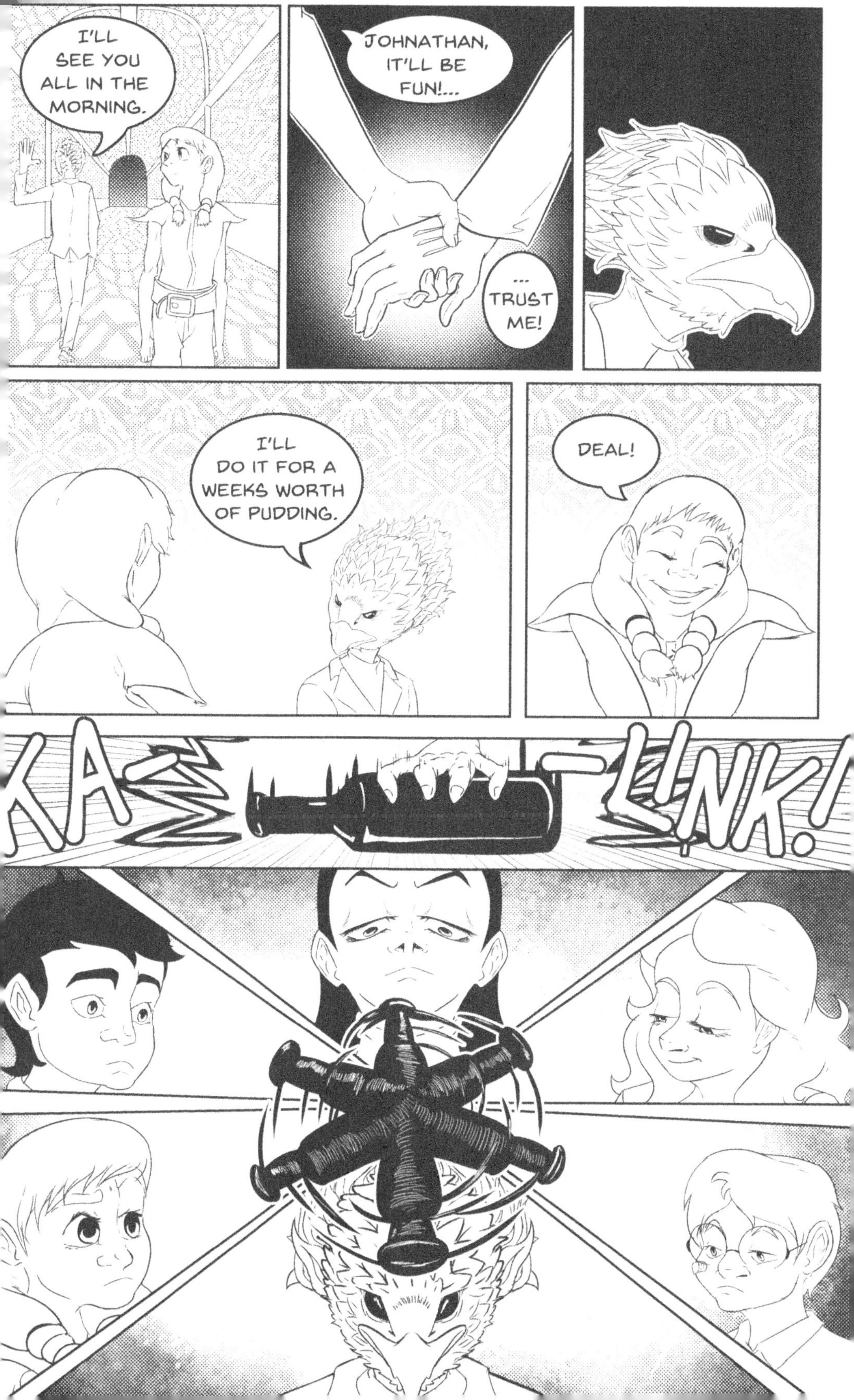
I'LL SEE YOU ALL IN THE MORNING.
JOHNATHAN, IT'LL BE FUN!...
... TRUST ME!
I'LL DO IT FOR A WEEKS WORTH OF PUDDING.
DEAL!
KA-LINK!

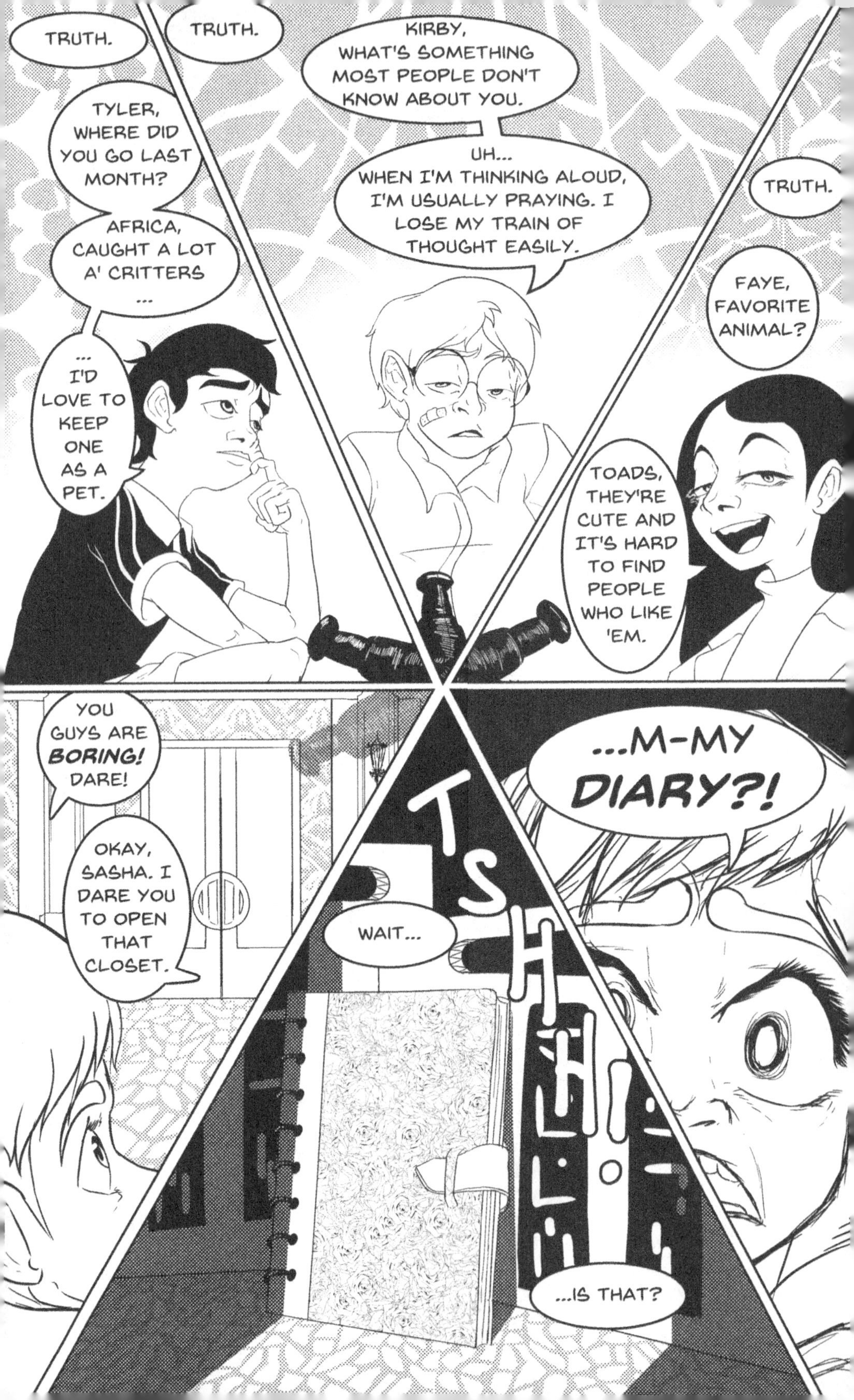
TRUTH.
TYLER, WHERE DID YOU GO LAST MONTH?
AFRICA, CAUGHT A LOT A' CRITTERS ...
... I'D LOVE TO KEEP ONE AS A PET.
TRUTH.
KIRBY, WHAT'S SOMETHING MOST PEOPLE DON'T KNOW ABOUT YOU.
UH... WHEN I'M THINKING ALOUD, I'M USUALLY PRAYING. I LOSE MY TRAIN OF THOUGHT EASILY.
TRUTH.
FAYE, FAVORITE ANIMAL?
TOADS, THEY'RE CUTE AND IT'S HARD TO FIND PEOPLE WHO LIKE 'EM.
YOU GUYS ARE *BORING!* DARE!
OKAY, SASHA. I DARE YOU TO OPEN THAT CLOSET.
TSHH
WAIT...
...IS THAT?
...M-MY *DIARY?!*

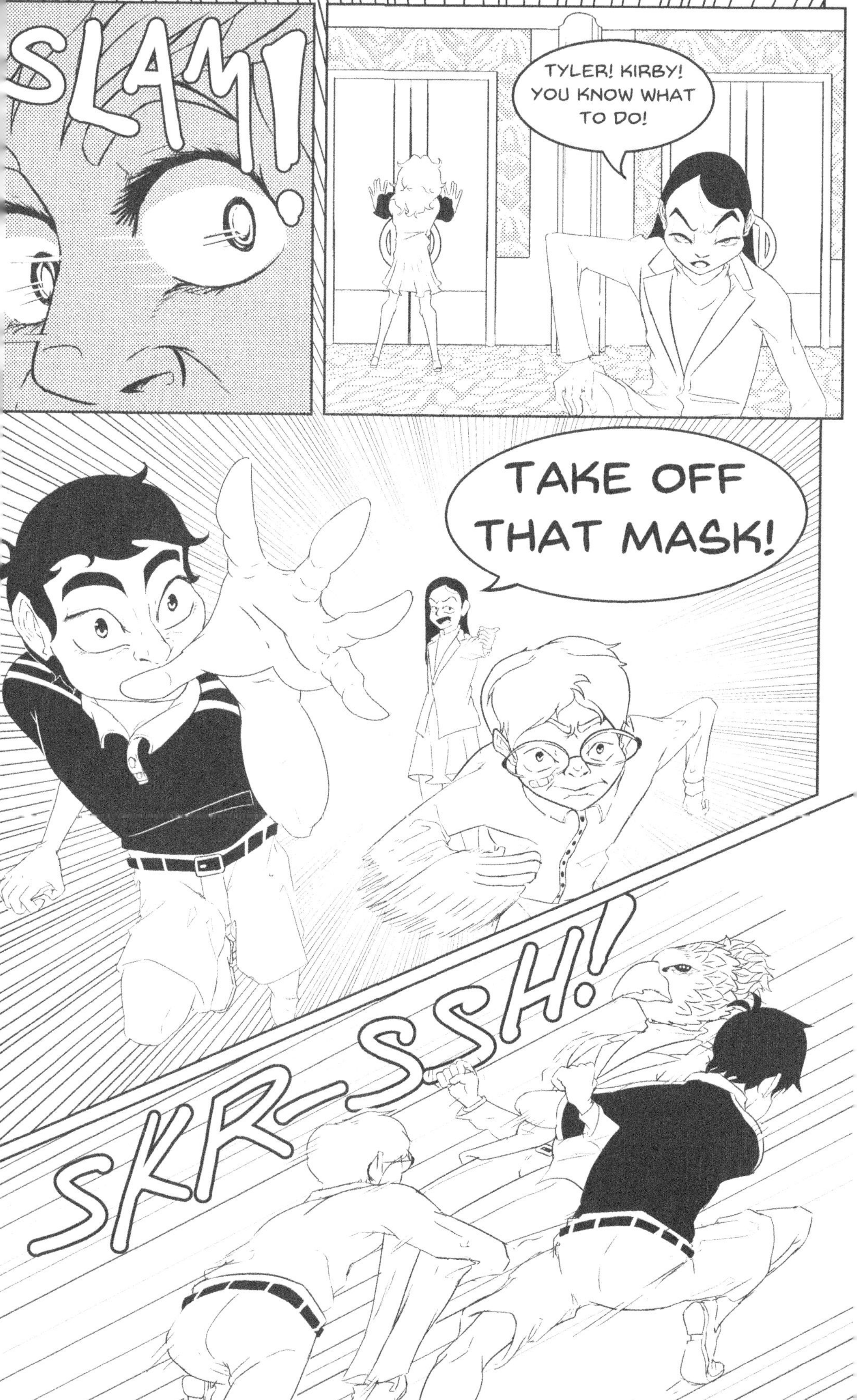
SLAM!
TYLER! KIRBY! YOU KNOW WHAT TO DO!
TAKE OFF THAT MASK!
SKR-SSH!

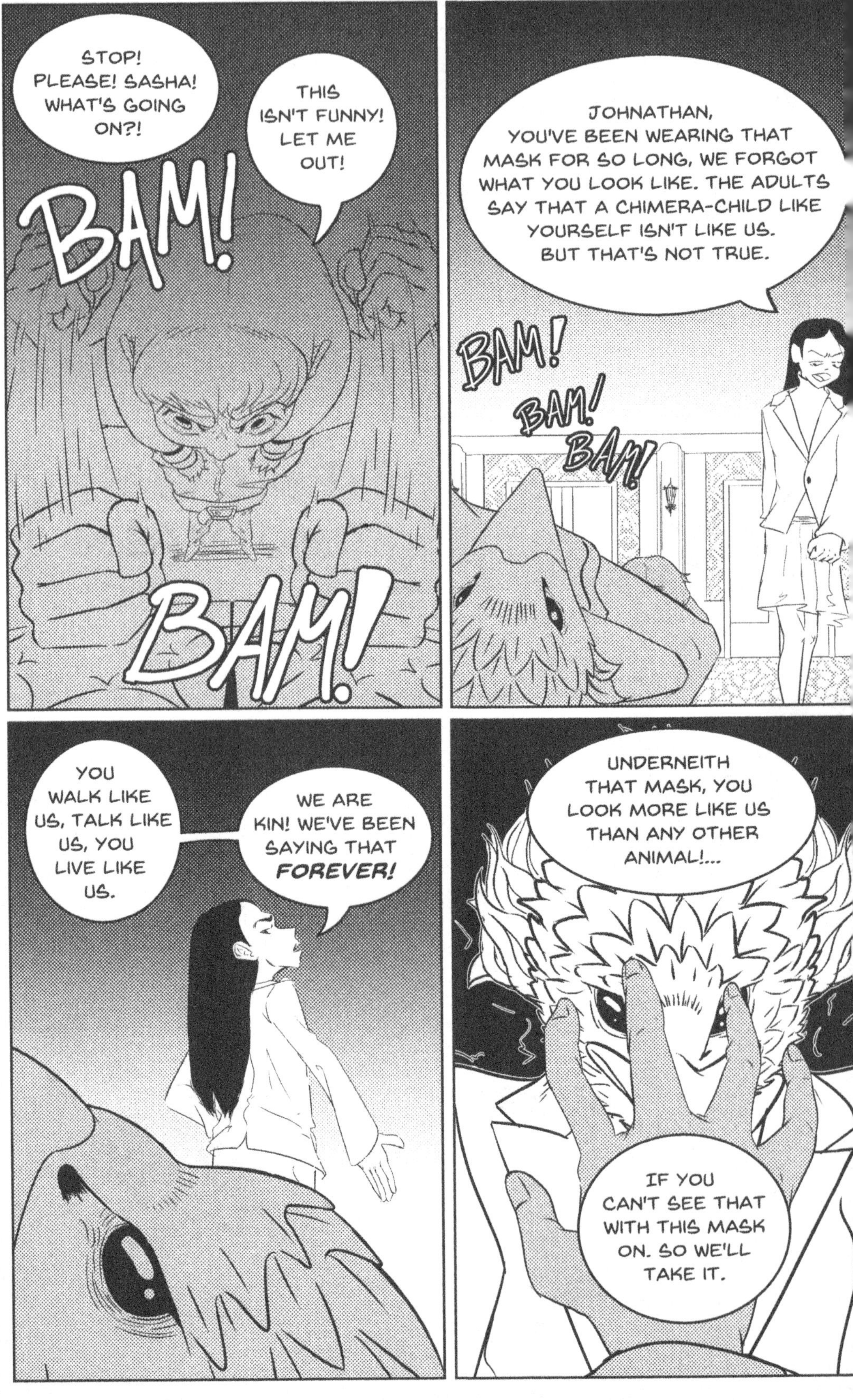
STOP! PLEASE! SASHA! WHAT'S GOING ON?!
THIS ISN'T FUNNY! LET ME OUT!
BAM!
BAM!
JOHNATHAN, YOU'VE BEEN WEARING THAT MASK FOR SO LONG, WE FORGOT WHAT YOU LOOK LIKE. THE ADULTS SAY THAT A CHIMERA-CHILD LIKE YOURSELF ISN'T LIKE US. BUT THAT'S NOT TRUE.
BAM!
BAM!
BAM!
YOU WALK LIKE US, TALK LIKE US, YOU LIVE LIKE US.
WE ARE KIN! WE'VE BEEN SAYING THAT FOREVER!
UNDERNEITH THAT MASK, YOU LOOK MORE LIKE US THAN ANY OTHER ANIMAL!...
IF YOU CAN'T SEE THAT WITH THIS MASK ON. SO WE'LL TAKE IT.

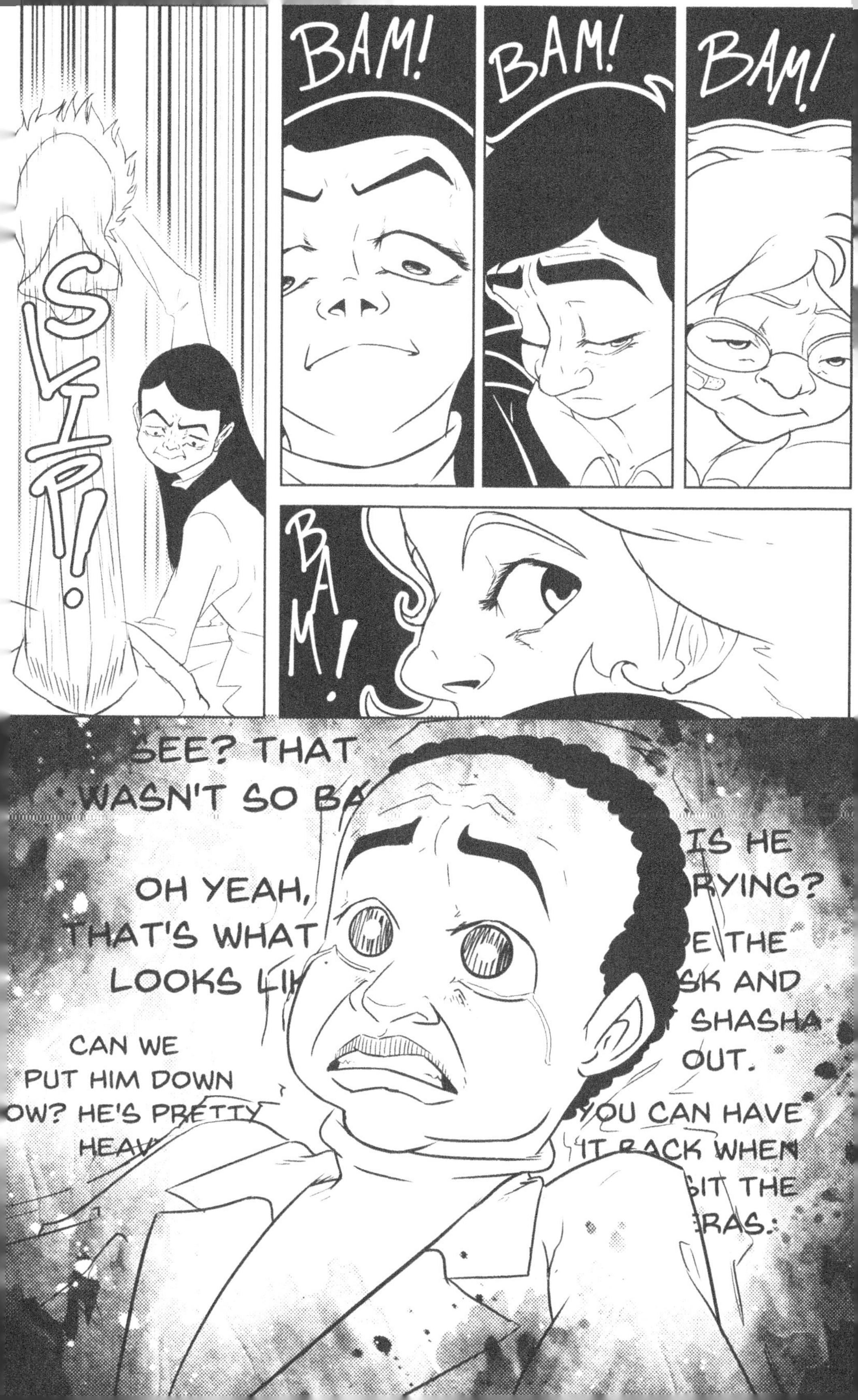

SLIP!
BAM!
BAM!
BAM!
BAM!
SEE? THAT WASN'T SO BA
IS HE RYING?
OH YEAH, THAT'S WHAT LOOKS LI
E THE SK AND SHASHA OUT.
CAN WE PUT HIM DOWN OW? HE'S PRETTY HEAV
YOU CAN HAVE IT BACK WHEN SIT THE ERAS.

...
JONATHAN?!
HELLO,
RUDY.
TSK!

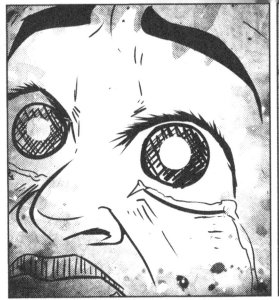

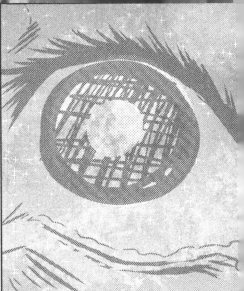

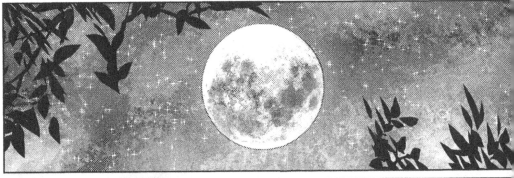

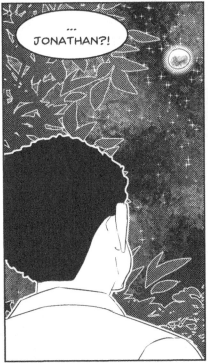

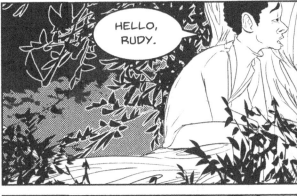

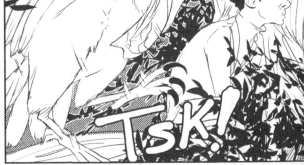

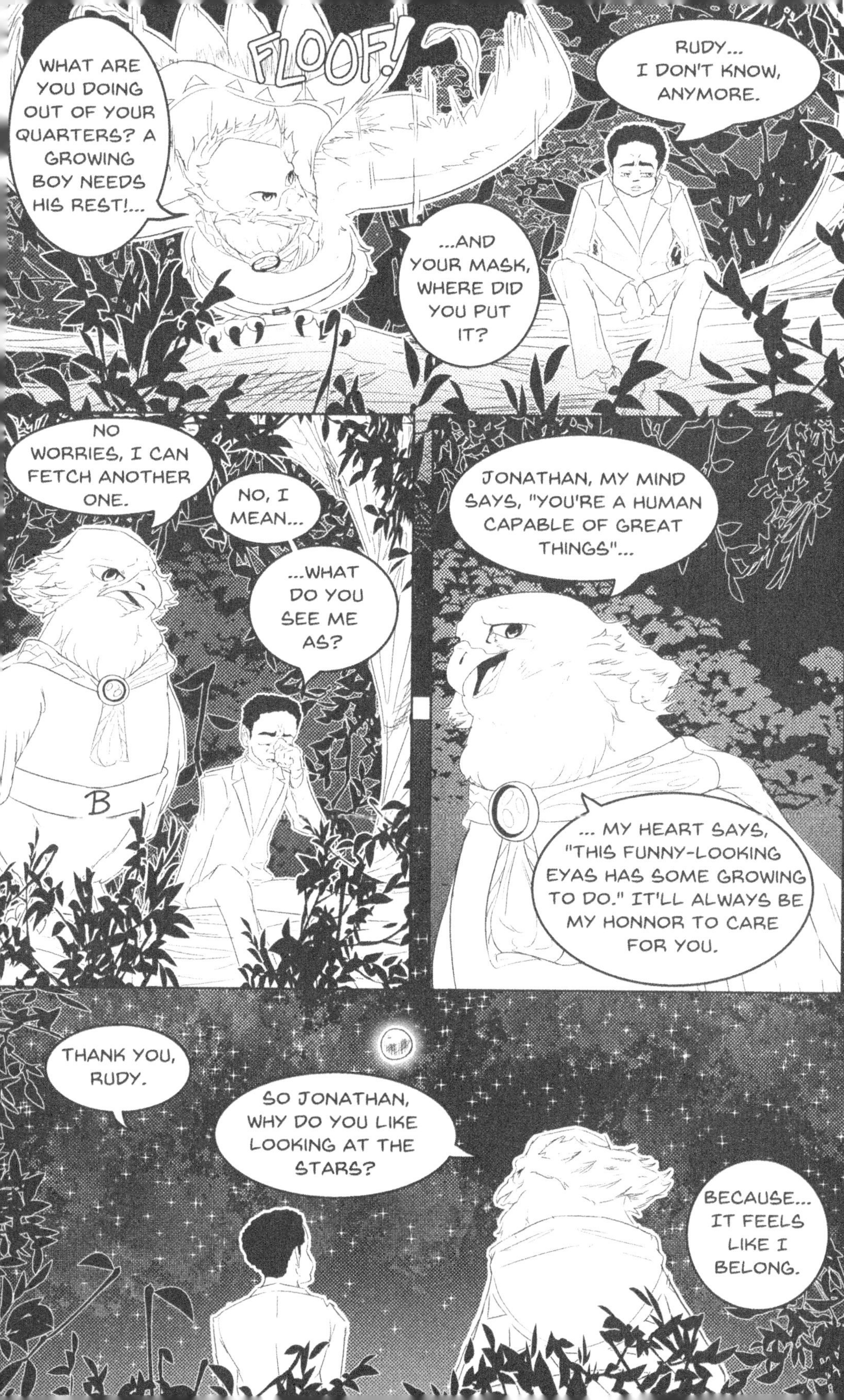
FLOOF!
WHAT ARE YOU DOING OUT OF YOUR QUARTERS? A GROWING BOY NEEDS HIS REST!...
...AND YOUR MASK, WHERE DID YOU PUT IT?
RUDY... I DON'T KNOW, ANYMORE.
NO WORRIES, I CAN FETCH ANOTHER ONE.
NO, I MEAN...
...WHAT DO YOU SEE ME AS?
B
JONATHAN, MY MIND SAYS, "YOU'RE A HUMAN CAPABLE OF GREAT THINGS"...
... MY HEART SAYS, "THIS FUNNY-LOOKING EYAS HAS SOME GROWING TO DO." IT'LL ALWAYS BE MY HONNOR TO CARE FOR YOU.
THANK YOU, RUDY.
SO JONATHAN, WHY DO YOU LIKE LOOKING AT THE STARS?
BECAUSE... IT FEELS LIKE I BELONG.

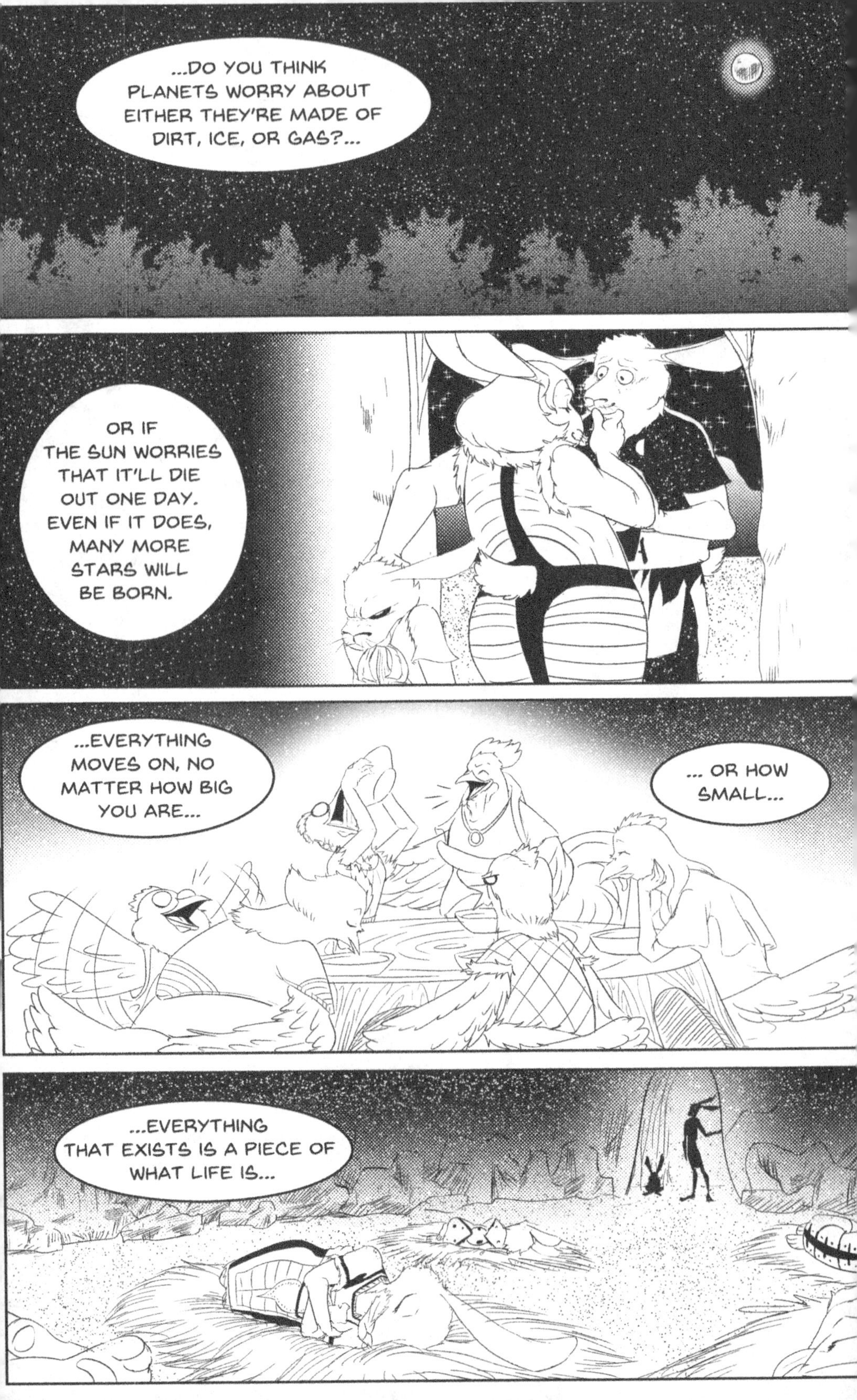
...DO YOU THINK PLANETS WORRY ABOUT EITHER THEY'RE MADE OF DIRT, ICE, OR GAS?...
OR IF THE SUN WORRIES THAT IT'LL DIE OUT ONE DAY. EVEN IF IT DOES, MANY MORE STARS WILL BE BORN.
...EVERYTHING MOVES ON, NO MATTER HOW BIG YOU ARE...
... OR HOW SMALL...
...EVERYTHING THAT EXISTS IS A PIECE OF WHAT LIFE IS...

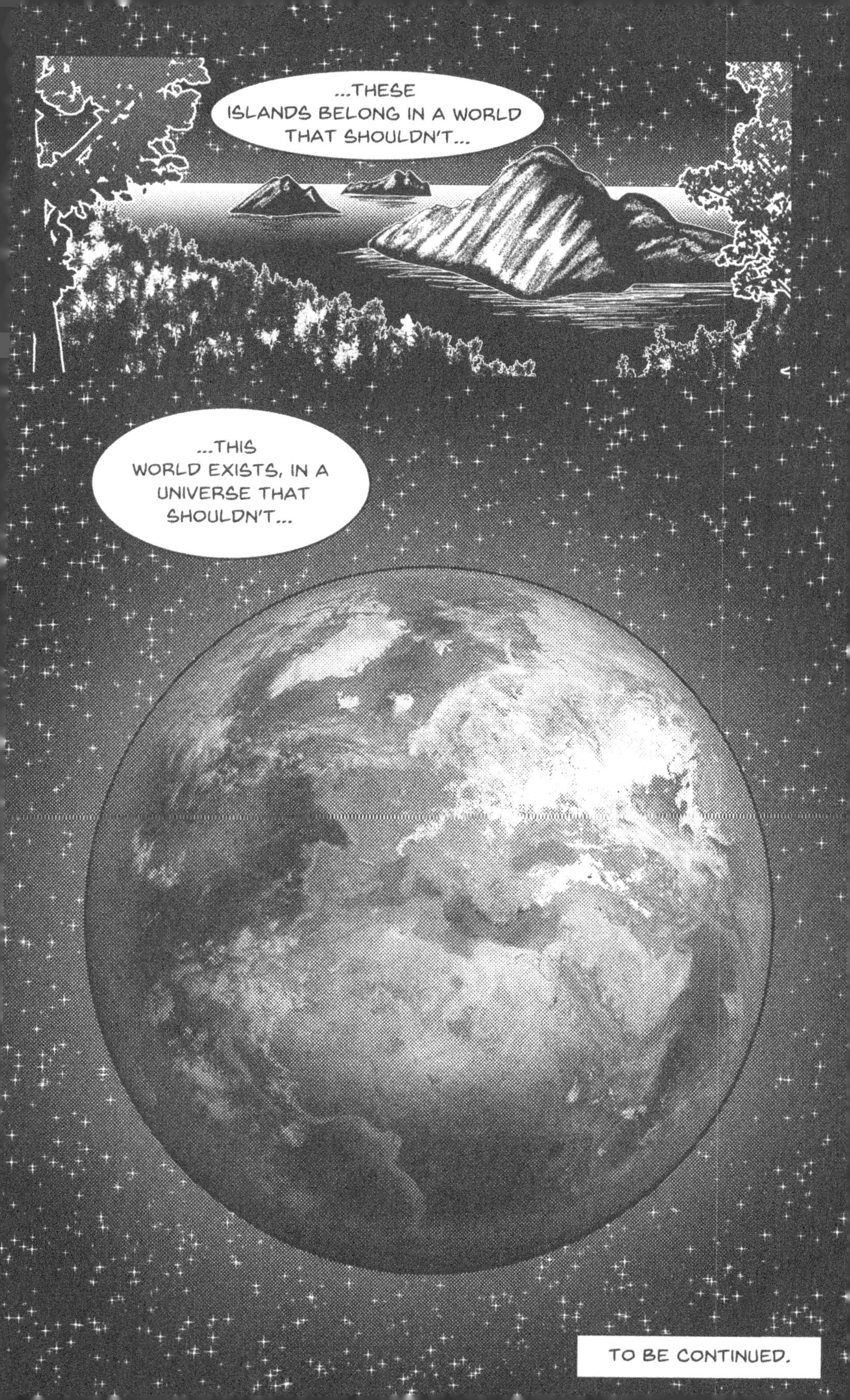
...THESE ISLANDS BELONG IN A WORLD THAT SHOULDN'T...
...THIS WORLD EXISTS, IN A UNIVERSE THAT SHOULDN'T...
TO BE CONTINUED.

AUTHOR NOTES

An appropriate beginning to this mini-documentary of creating this pilot is, "THANK YOU FOR READING THIS BOOK!" This is a world I've had on my mind way before Purgatory Academy and I finally have the confidence to tell it after rewriting the introductory chapter over and over again. When something doesn't sit right, a good idea is to look around and copy what you like.

The inspiration for this series is wanting to tell a generational story inspired by Hirohiko Araki's *Jojo's Bizzare Adventure*. But instead of following the bloodline of a specific family, it follows the bloodline of significant characters of the Chimerian race. The setting is heavily inspired by Irrational Game's Bioshock series, and the art was inspired by Yoshihiro Togashi's *HUNTER×HUNTER*. What I wanted to do stylistically was to have simple characters stand out against detailed backgrounds. The backgrounds were a huge change of pace because after working on Purgatory Academy, where the majority of backgrounds are interiors, I was able to draw more exteriors with this series. That was only the beginning of the changes that I noticed when working on this.

If my first Book, Purgatory Academy: Book 1, was me figuring out if I was good at making comics, and my second, Purgatory Academy: Book 2, was improving on the first without limitations, then this book is taking what I've learned, limiting myself, and adding the challenge of making a good first
impression. Initially, I wanted to make the introductory chapter around 15-20 pages so I've written two scripts to get the ball rolling in my mind. This was around the time I was drawing chapters for Book 2. As I was gaining experience working on Book 2, I was slowly developing character arcs, not just for Sarah, but the people she would associate with to the point that she wasn't THE main character, but one of many in this world.

For the direction I wanted to go with this series, I settled on 4 characters; Sarah, Ruth, Odd, and Jonathan. The goal is to let the audience know what each character wants, their drawbacks, their personality, and their relation to the world all in 10 pages with 2 pages in between to change perspective. When I finally settled on a template to structure this book, the rest was just execution.

THE WORLD

I gotta say I couldn't tell you what the world visually looked like until I had to draw it. And when I drew the cityscape, I used it as a map for later parts. What I already had down was the location, what kind of people would be living there, and why they would live there, but just not what it looked like. I believe I recorded the majority of this project on YouTube and you could hear me adding ideas to the world as I draw the background or write impromptu dialogue. At the end of the day, all the changes needed to make sense within the world and be presented to the audience.

I had several general themes that were always going to be a part of the major story such as a diverse cast of animals and a caste system within their society. Within any society, especially a diverse one, I see that there will always be inequality but in this specific setting, the characters focus more on their purpose within their society instead of having a need to change it. The two goals I had for the world are to act as the intro, the interlude between the character plots, and the outro as well as show how this unknown island maintains balance.

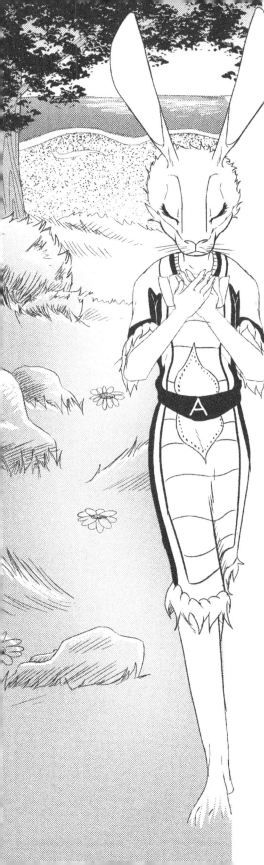

SARAH

The concept of Chimera Island started with Sarah so it's fitting to have her be the first character the audience sees. I imagine Sarah as a character not needing to speak to people unless she needs to.

I was initially inspired by Northwest Coast/Alaskan native art when designing her dress and thought I would pull from that idea when I would illustrate the world she lived in. That was until I got to the twelfth page and decided to subvert expectations and change to a more metropolitan setting. That twelfth page gave me visual grounding on how the world may operate outside of dialogue. The story I wanted to tell with her 10 pages was, "Girl embraces wilderness to achieve her goal."

Since she doesn't talk unless she feels she needs to, the scenario that I went with is effective to catch a reader's attention, build curiosity on how she's got herself in this situation, identify her goal, and see what lengths she's willing to take to achieve her goal. Then subvert the reader's expectation of what the setting is.

RUTH

The main inspiration for Ruth's story was inspired by a friend's experience of identifying friends from acquaintances. The main thing I wanted to avoid was making anybody antagonistic for the sake of it or solely for the fact that she bears a different letter than most. What made sense to me was how people's opinions can easily be swayed through popularity, numbers, and/or influence. I don't see it as a good or bad thing, just a product of being social creatures.

This is also the part where I dropped the idea that everyone would wear a similar style of clothing as Sarah. To be honest, half the fun is trying out one-off styles and patterns for background characters and seeing what mentally sticks. I was inspired by looking at the clothing from Araki's Jojo's Bizzare Adventure series. It just makes sense for extremely different body types and creatures would try out something wacky from time to time.

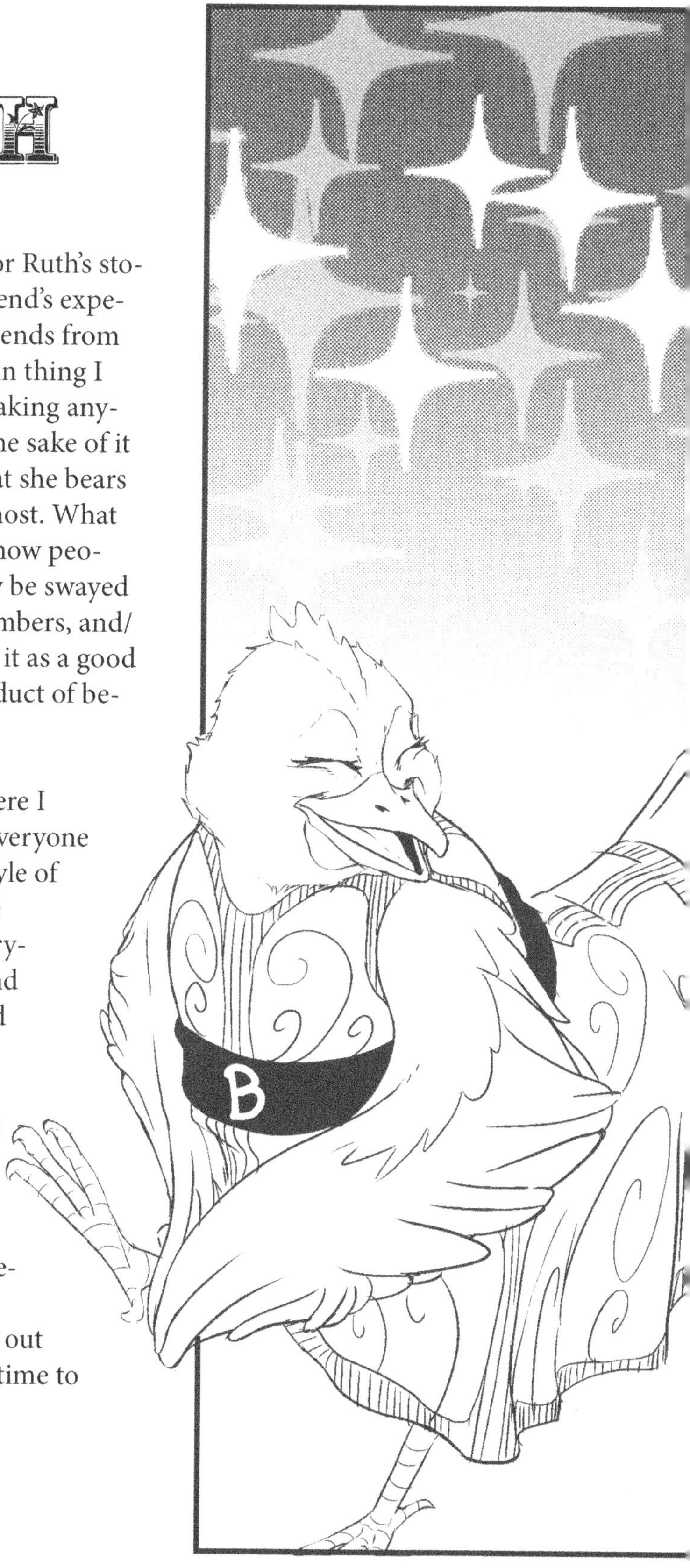

B

 ODD

I wanted to introduce Odd similarly to Ruth and opposite to Sarah. Similar to Ruth because he's also an outcast, not by the sign he bears, but by the profession of his mother. While Sarah is an active force in her own plot, Odd is reactive. The idea I wanted to get across with Odd is that he wants to be normal but he's born into taboos. Personally, this part was a mixed bag because there were sections that I really visually enjoyed like the fighting but this is also the part where I started to fear that there were too many things going on without a moment to rest. Within the script for this book, I had that in mind because I included two slow parts to establish Odd and Reggie's relationship.

Another interesting thing to note is the age of the audience reading the book. Because this part of the book revolves around Odd's relationship with his mother, and to an extent, her profession, I wanted to write this in a way that I would feel comfortable knowing an audience under 14 years may read this. After selling Purgatory Academy at physical locations and seeing people younger than the main characters saying they've read and enjoyed the book is nice to hear but then I realize the edgy jokes I included leave me with an uncomfortable feeling.

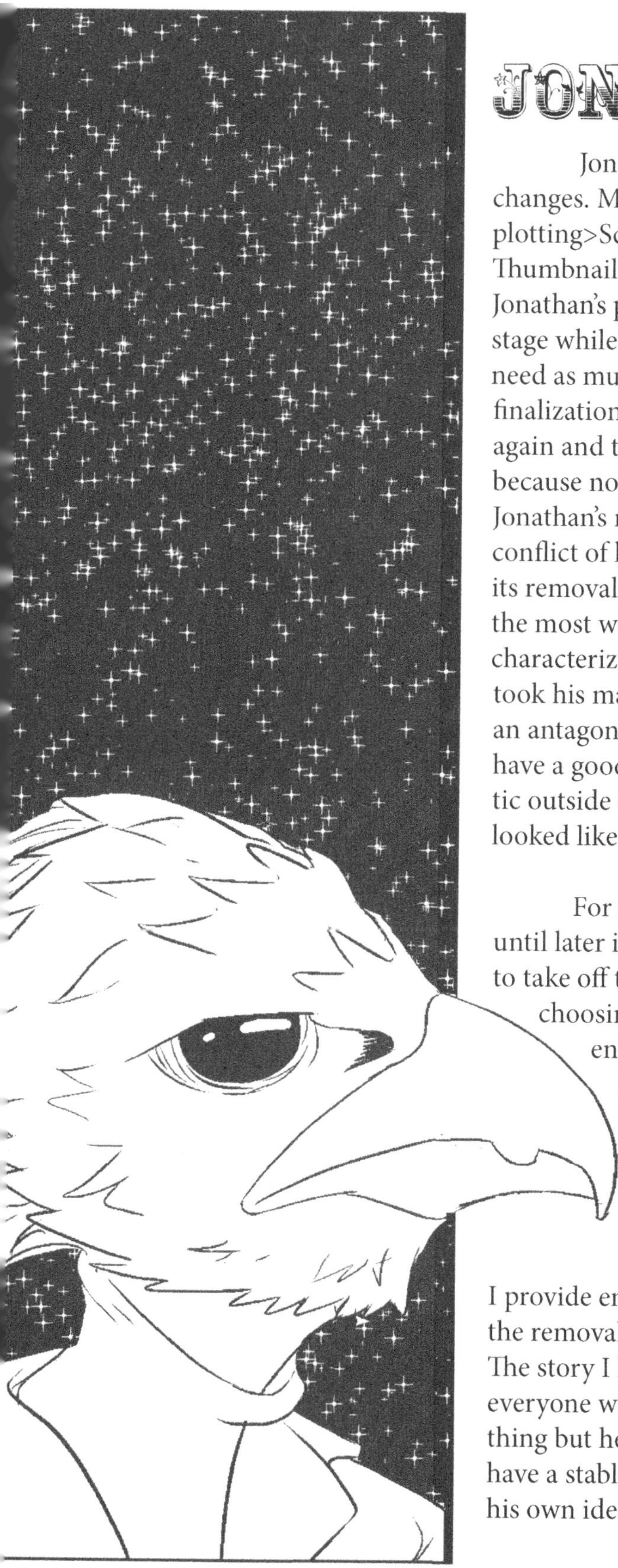

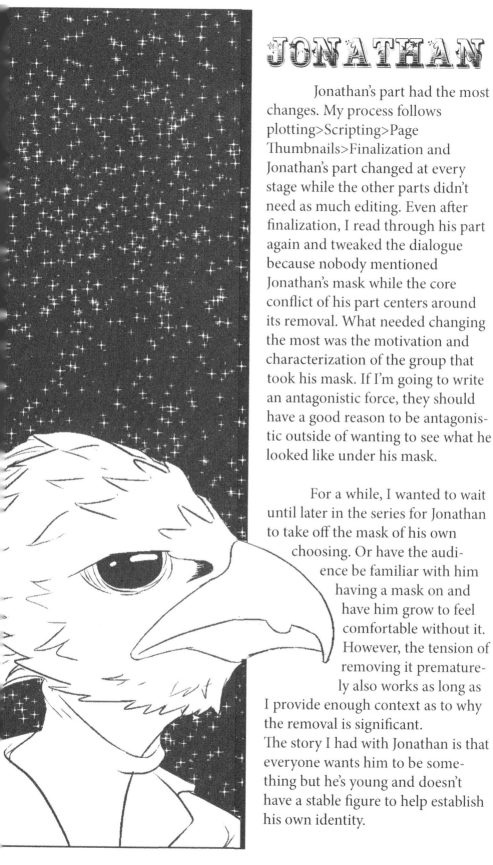

JONATHAN

Jonathan's part had the most changes. My process follows plotting>Scripting>Page Thumbnails>Finalization and Jonathan's part changed at every stage while the other parts didn't need as much editing. Even after finalization, I read through his part again and tweaked the dialogue because nobody mentioned Jonathan's mask while the core conflict of his part centers around its removal. What needed changing the most was the motivation and characterization of the group that took his mask. If I'm going to write an antagonistic force, they should have a good reason to be antagonistic outside of wanting to see what he looked like under his mask.

For a while, I wanted to wait until later in the series for Jonathan to take off the mask of his own choosing. Or have the audience be familiar with him having a mask on and have him grow to feel comfortable without it. However, the tension of removing it prematurely also works as long as I provide enough context as to why the removal is significant.
The story I had with Jonathan is that everyone wants him to be something but he's young and doesn't have a stable figure to help establish his own identity.

PRODUCTION SKETCHES

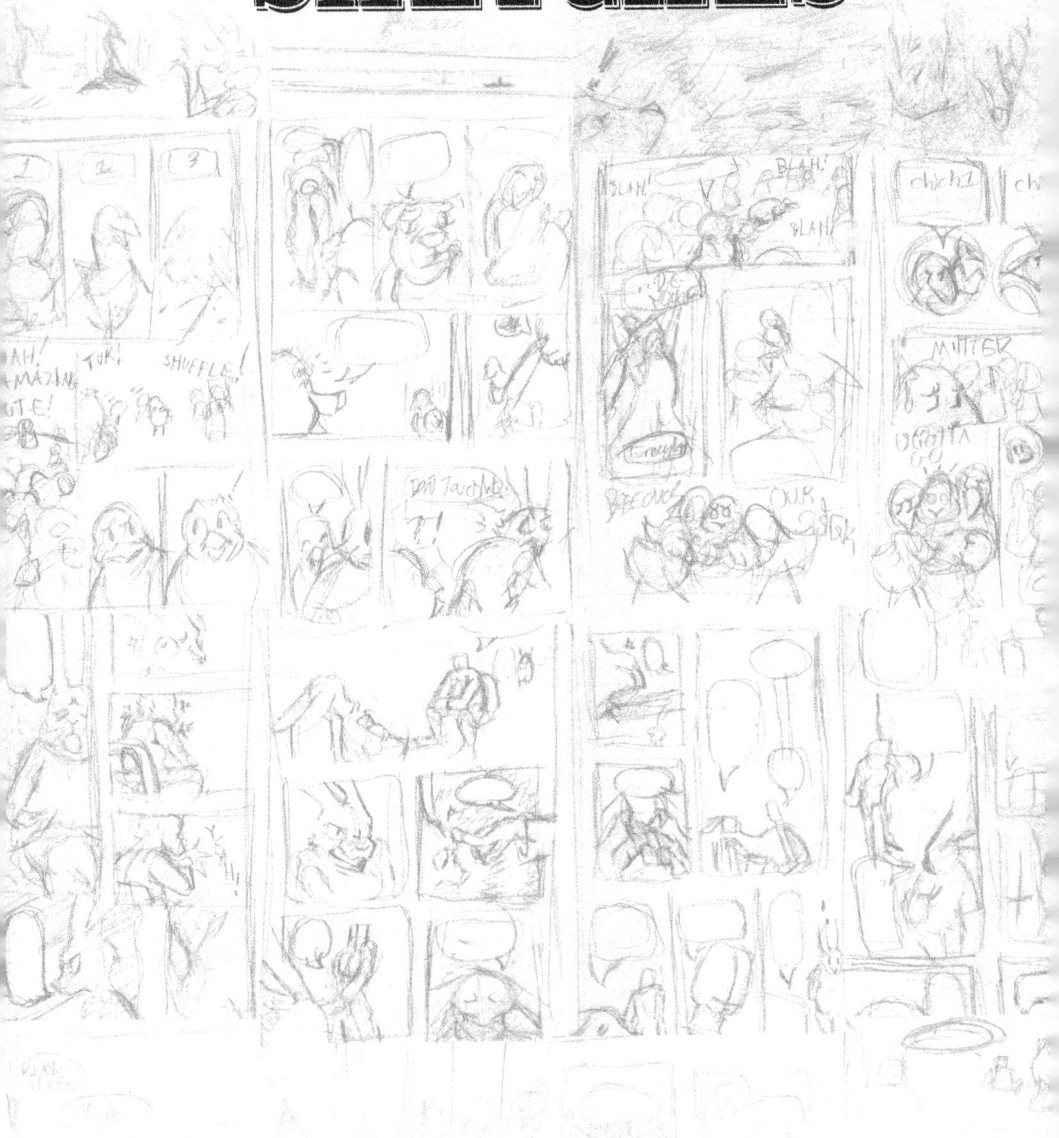

1
2
3
TUK!
SHUFFLE!
BLAH!
BLAH!
BLAH!

A showcase of the evolution of character designs and ideas. Any character not shown here is a safe assumption that either their designs were thought on the spot or haven't changed since conception.

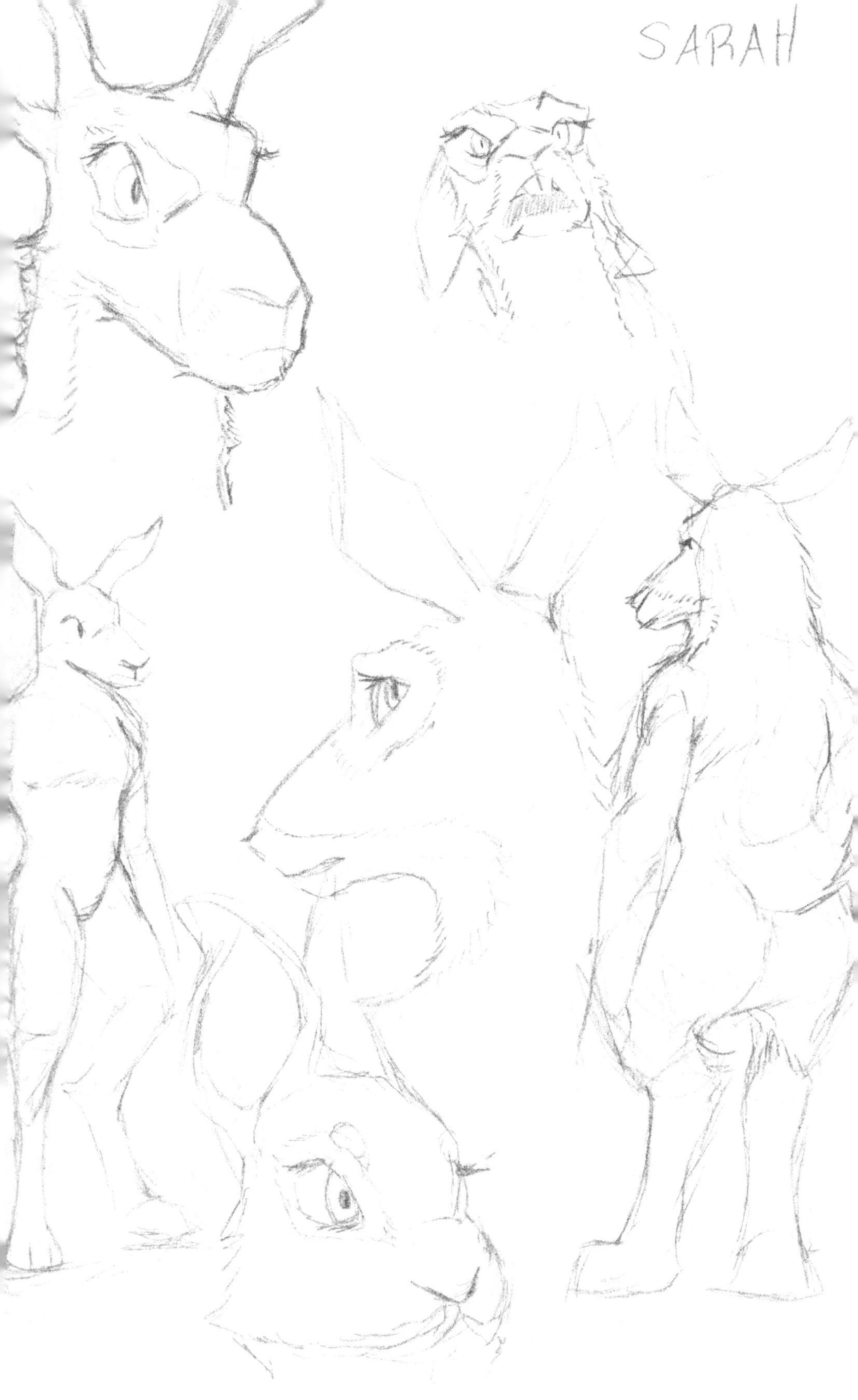
SARAH

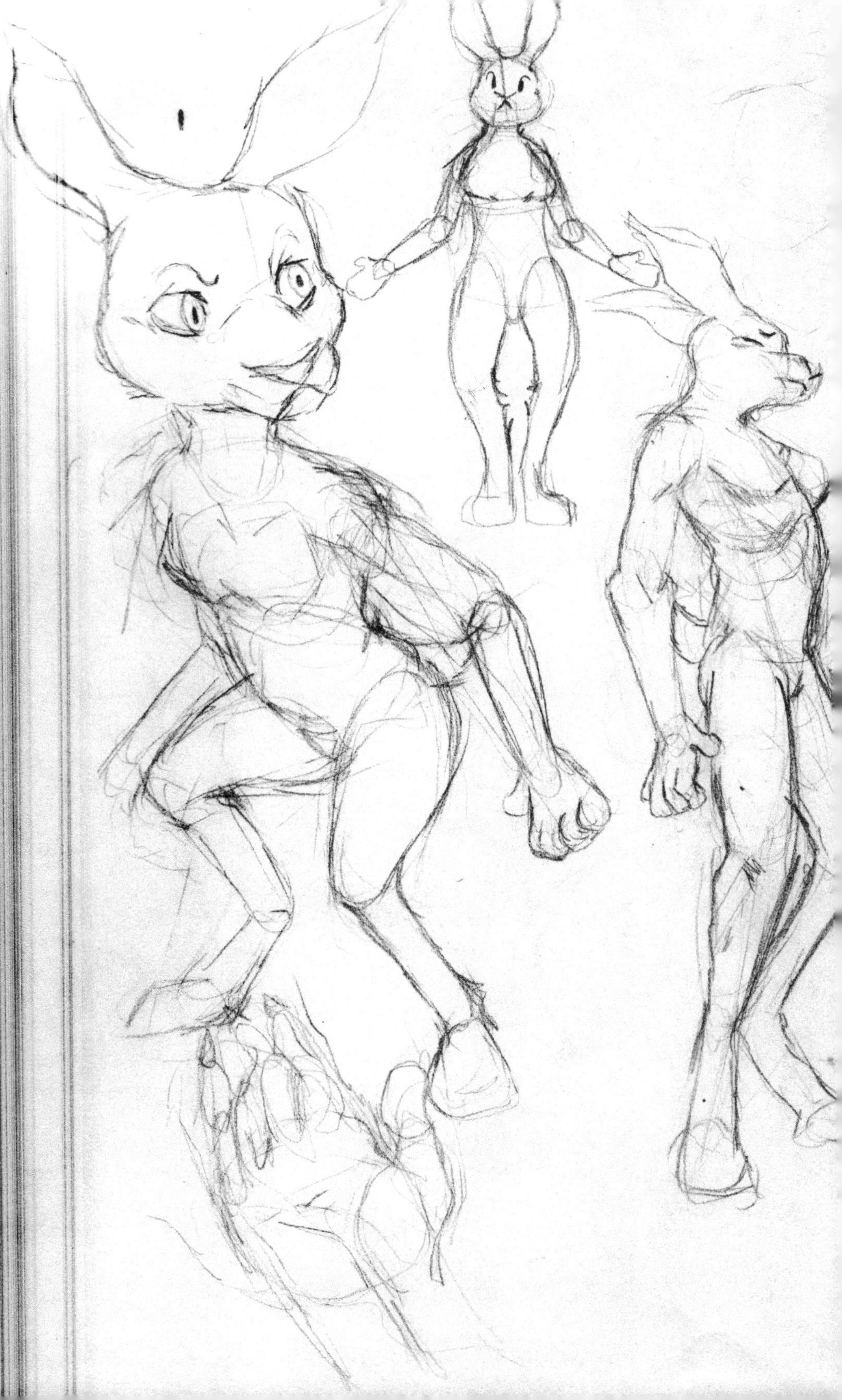

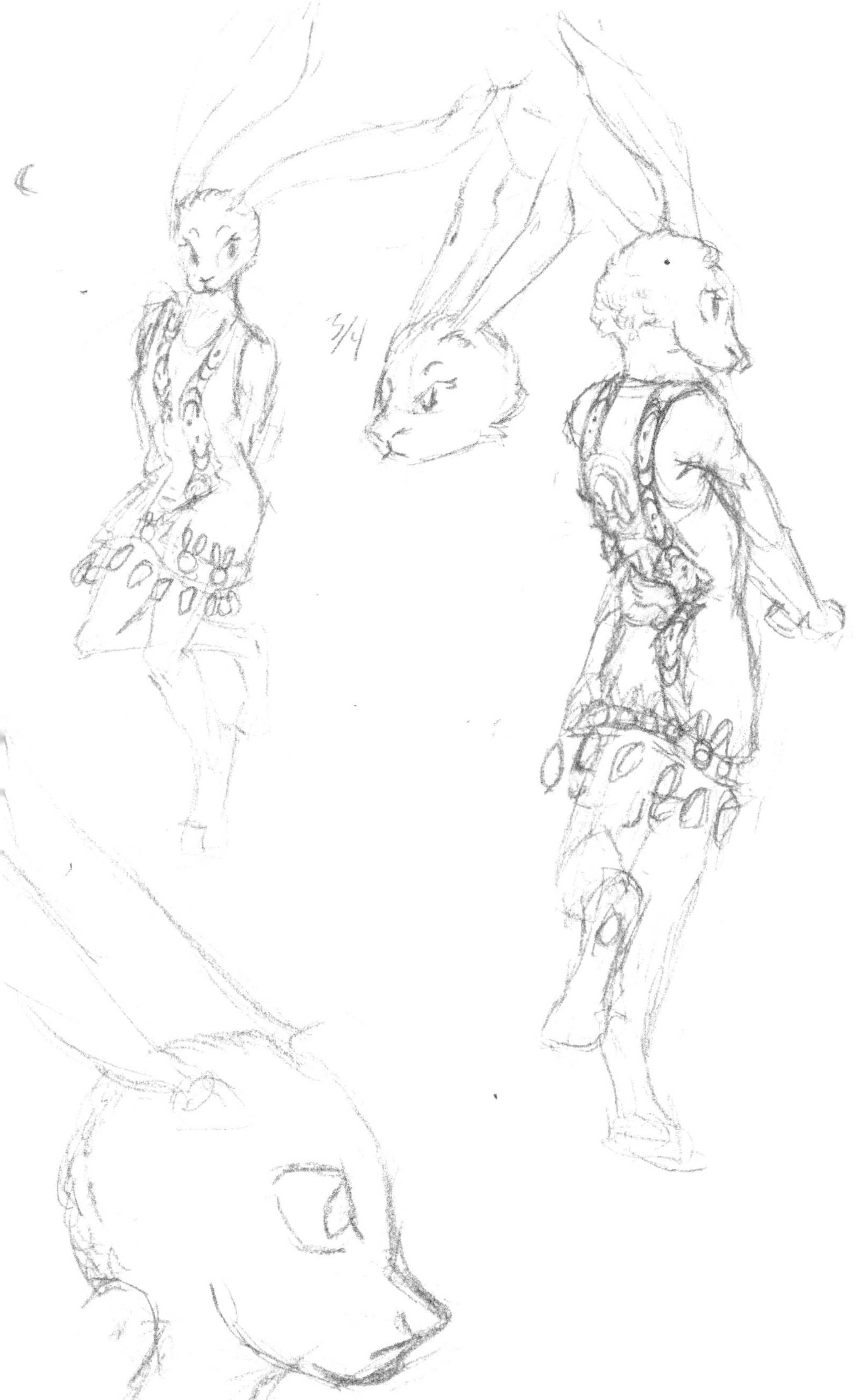
3/4

Ruth

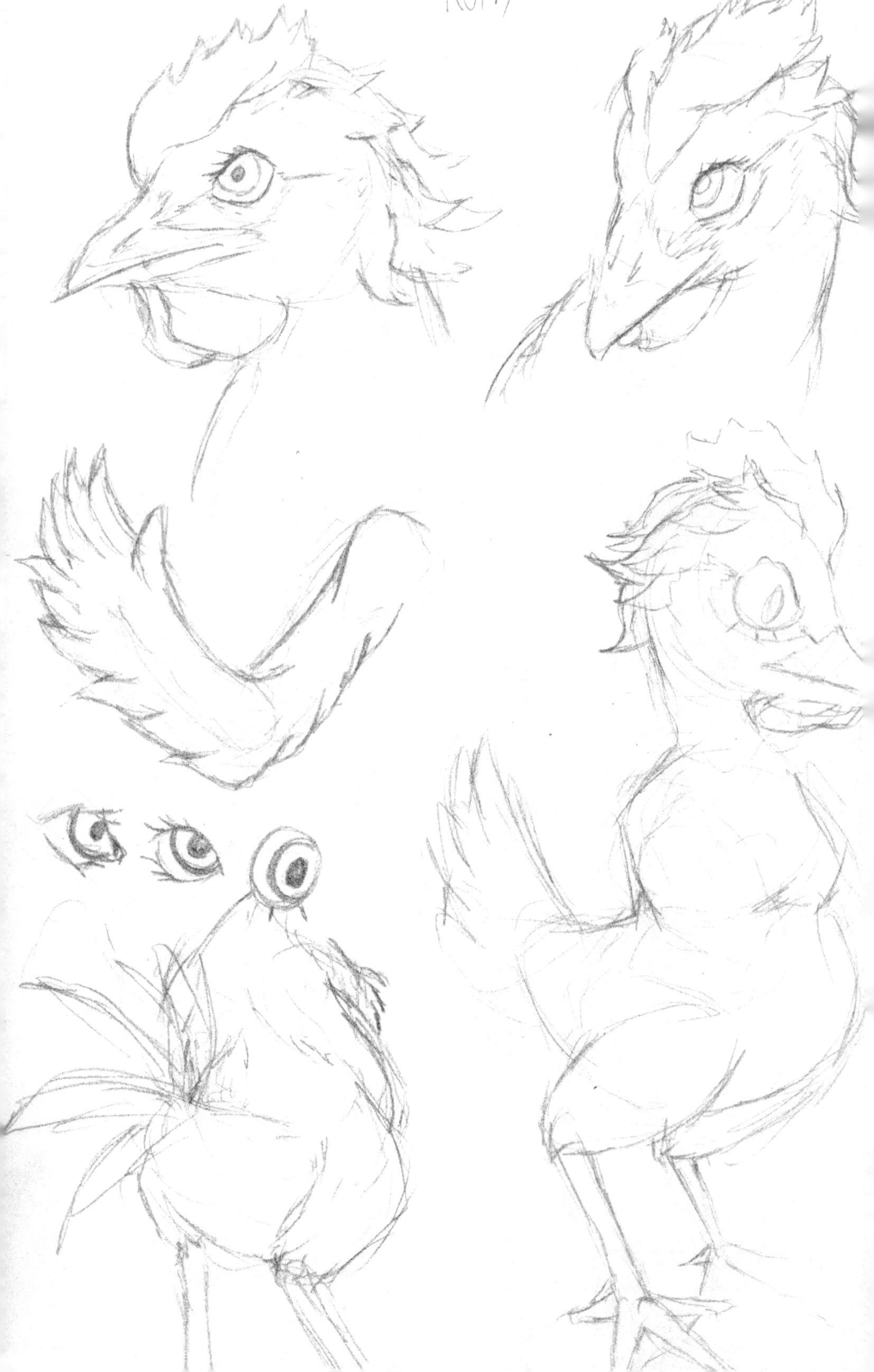

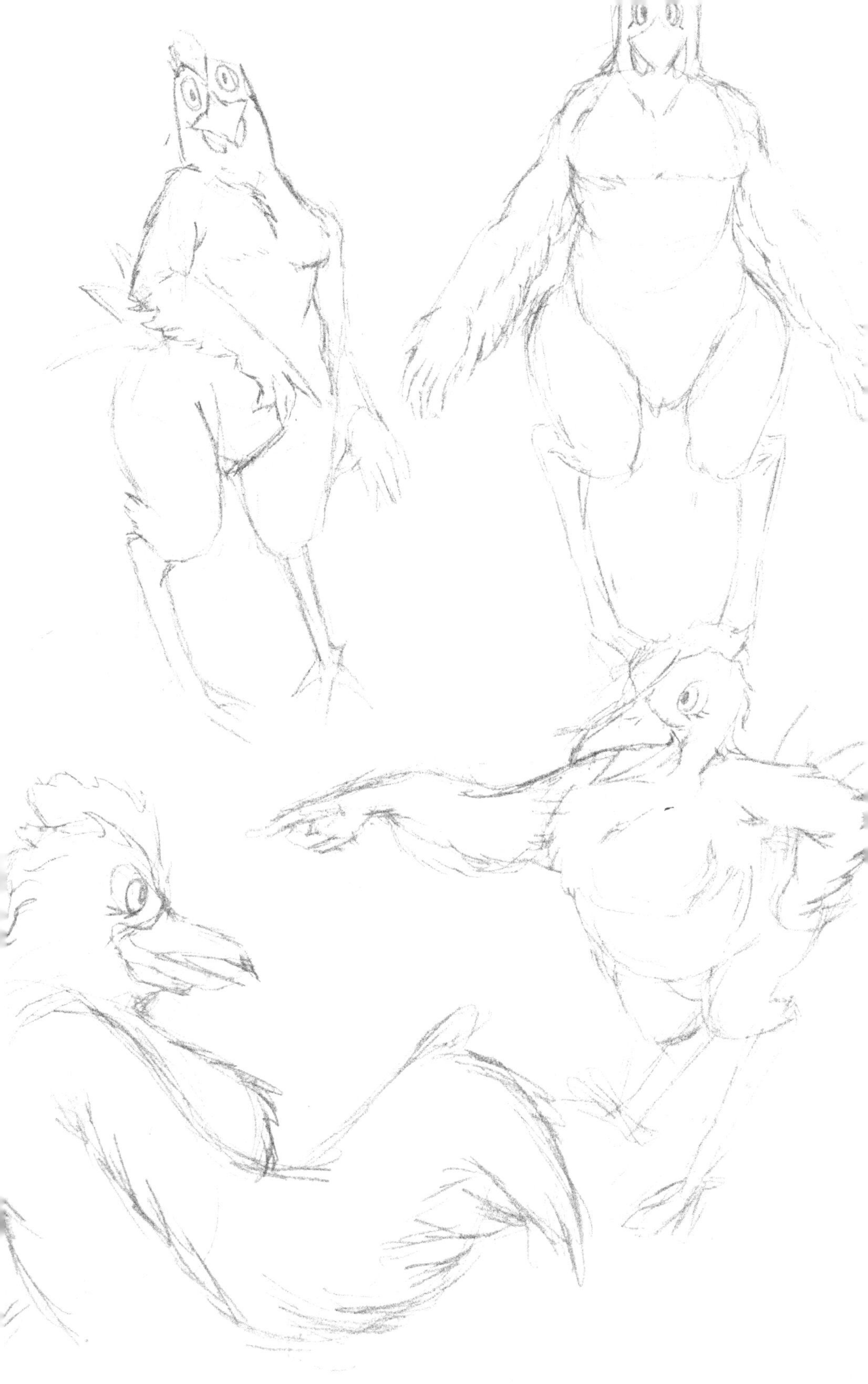

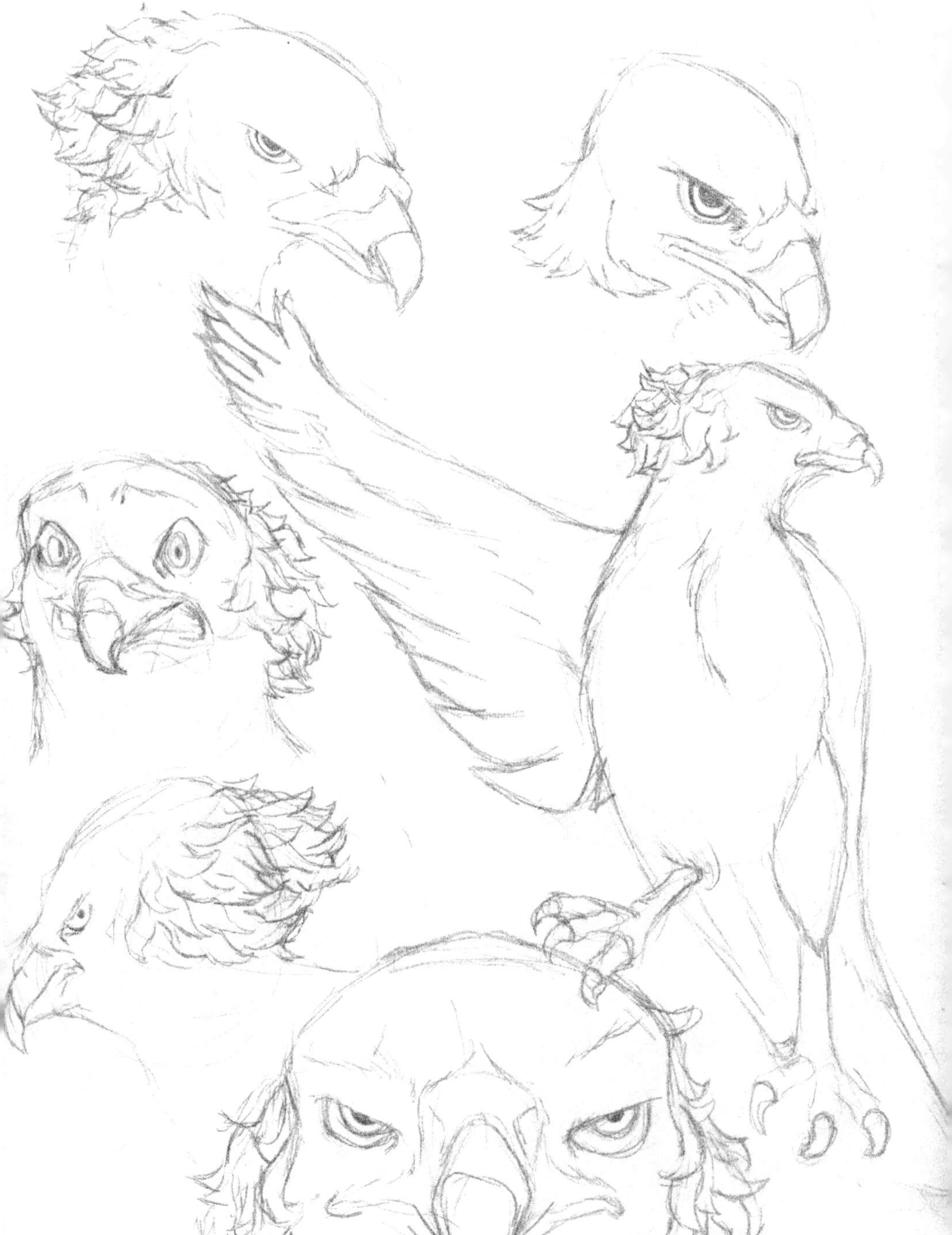

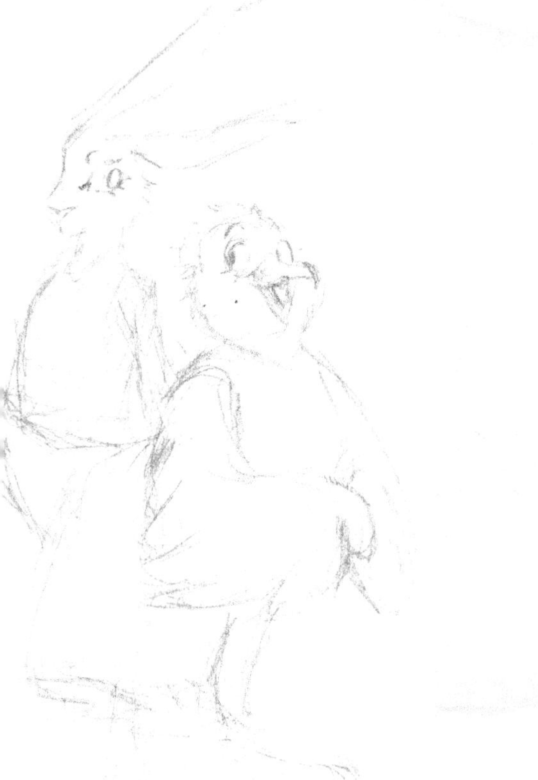
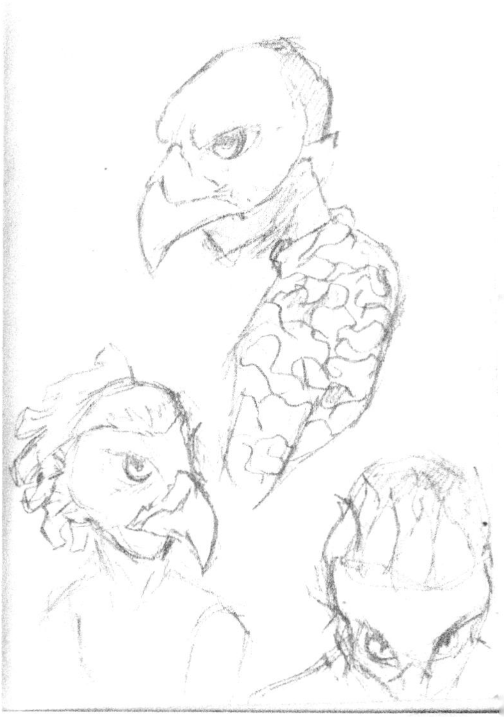
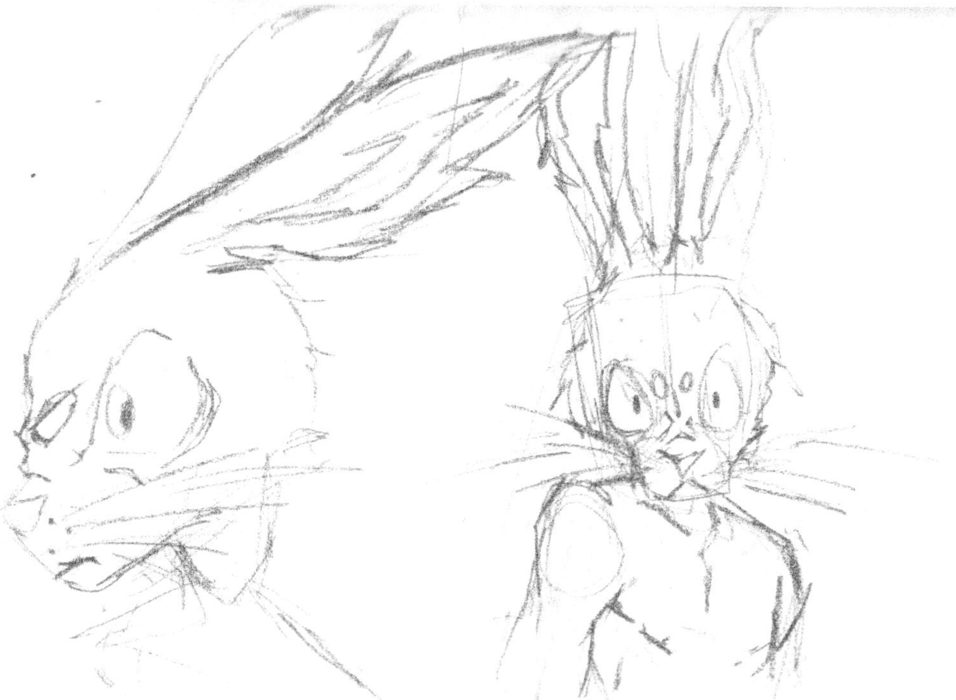

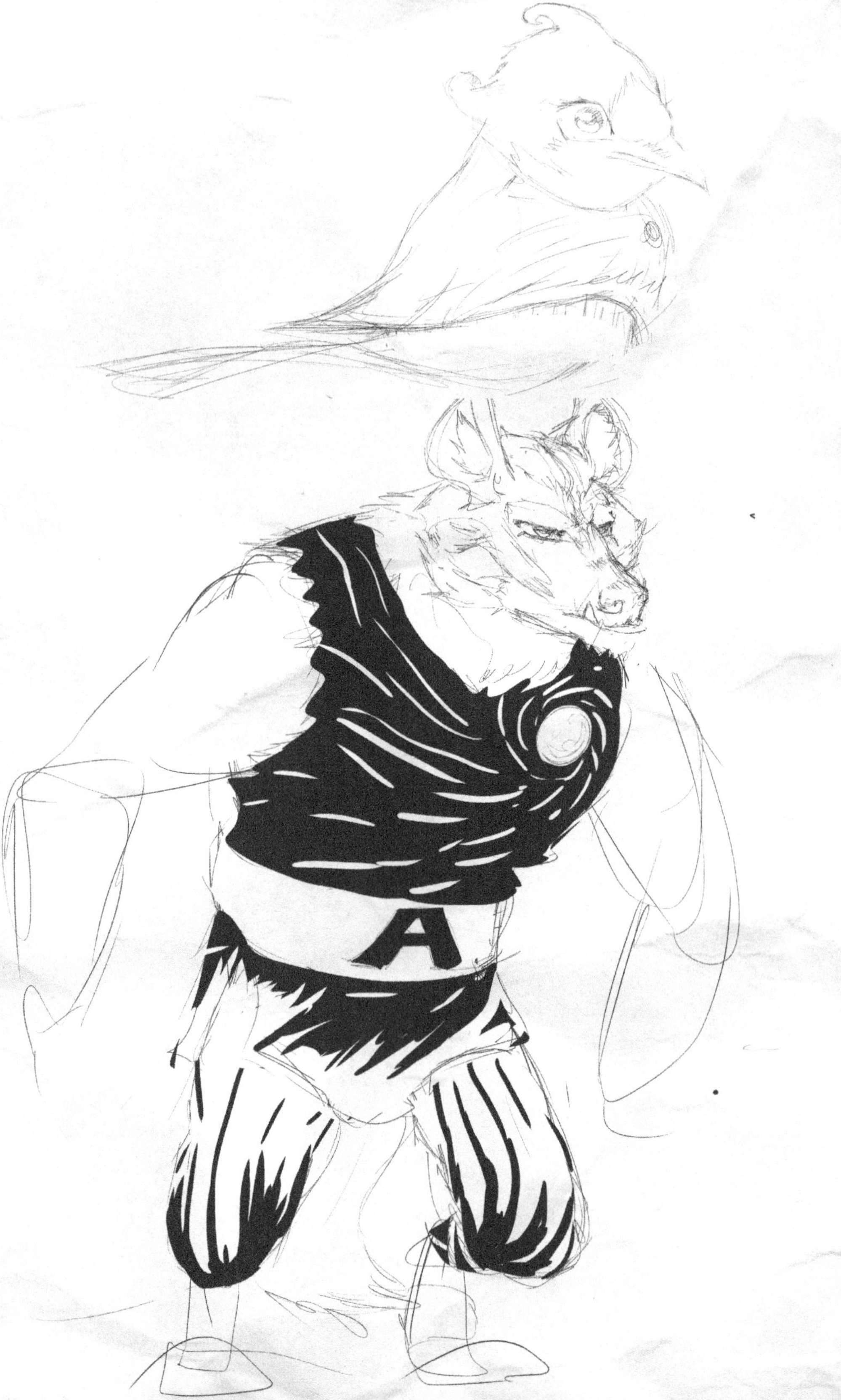
A

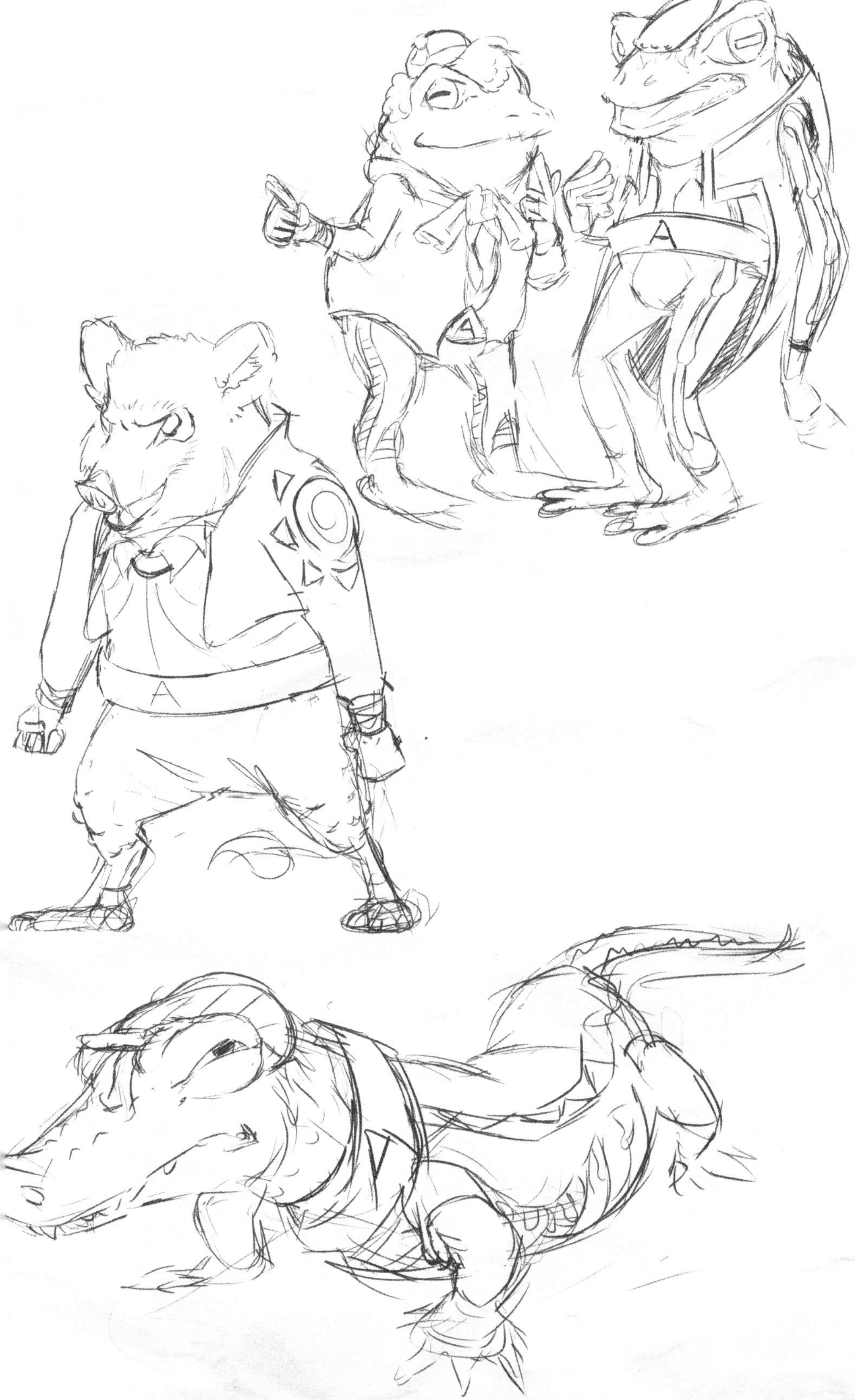

Jonathan

Faye

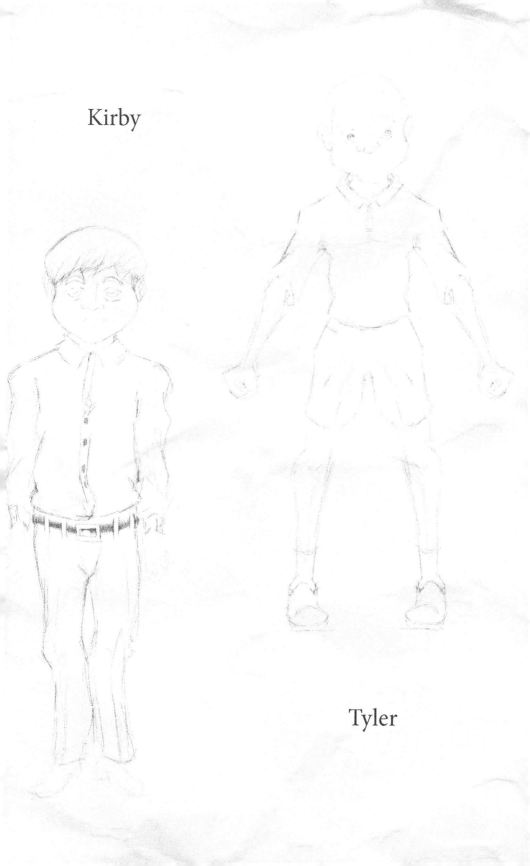

Kirby

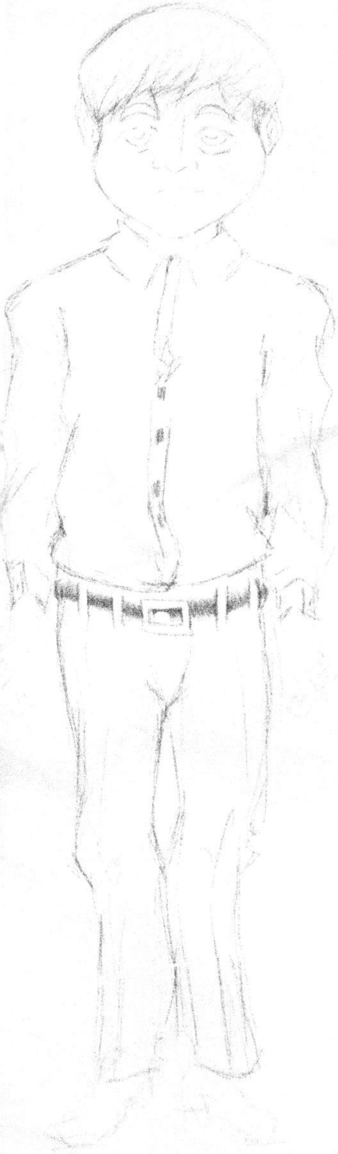

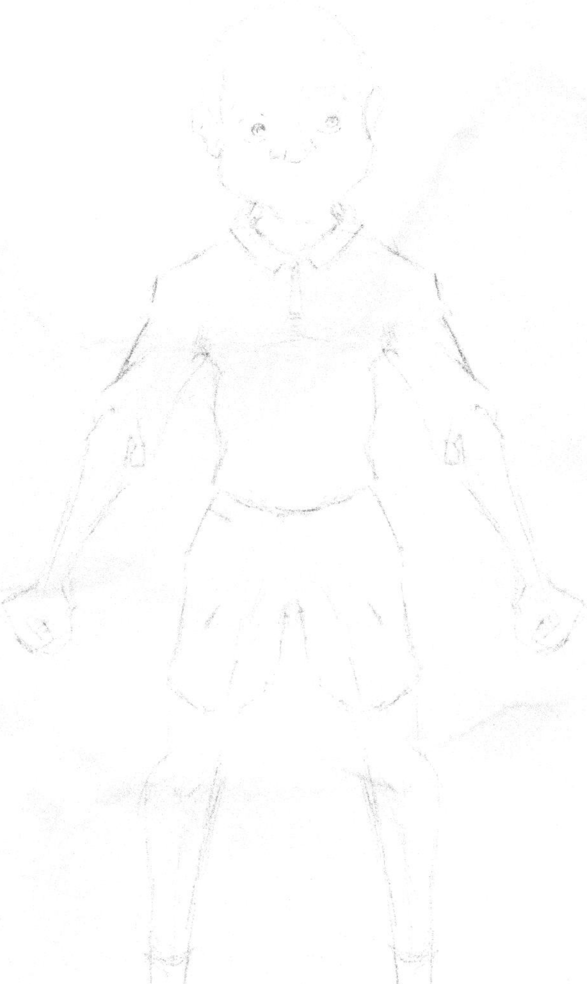

Tyler

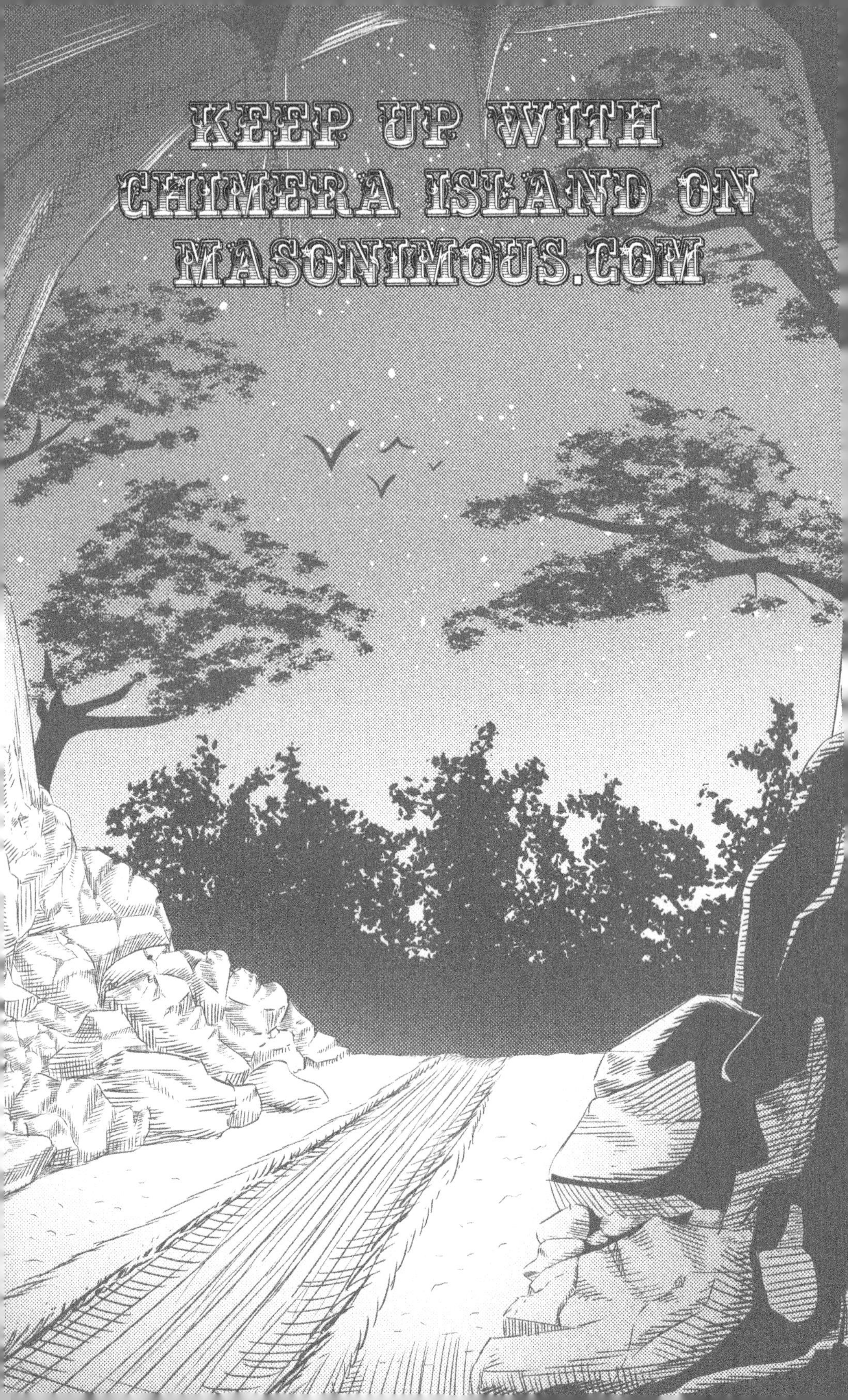
KEEP UP WITH CHIMERA ISLAND ON MASONIMOUS.COM

Made in the USA
Middletown, DE
27 October 2023

41325842R00040